A RECIPE for TROUBLE

A RECIPE for TROUBLE

SARAH TODD TAYLOR

First published in the UK in 2022 by Nosy Crow Ltd
The Crow's Nest, 14 Baden Place
Crosby Row, London, SE1 1YW, UK

Nosy Crow Eireann Ltd
44 Orchard Grove, Kenmare
Co Kerry, V93 FY22, Ireland

ISBN: 978 1 83994 095 8

A CIP catalogue record for this book is available from the British Library.

Printed and bound in the UK by Clays Ltd, Elcograf S.p.A.
Typeset by Tiger Media

Papers used by Nosy Crow are made from wood grown in sustainable forests

1 3 5 7 9 10 8 6 4 2

www.nosycrow.com

For Neil

A code for you to crack:
JODNINUOGWJOYJNCVX

CHAPTER
ONE

Alice stared at the Eiffel Tower and dared herself to add more fireworks. *There is always room for improvement*, she thought. She had spent all morning crafting icing into the city's most famous landmark for the top of an anniversary cake. Sugar strands criss-crossed one another in a perfect replica of the tower's girders. She had made the viewing platform in paper-thin sheets of caramel and added icing miniatures of the bride and groom, with the swirls on the woman's dress picked out in silver. It was gorgeous.

But not gorgeous enough for Alice. She had added spun-sugar orbs to look like fireworks exploding from the top of the tower, and now she decided that she could top even *this!*

Alice cupped the icing bag in one hand and leaned in close to one of the orbs of whisper-thin sugar strands. She held her breath and placed a small dot of glistening white icing on an individual strand. She gave a light twist and left a single star hanging from the wisp of sugar. Alice worked quickly, adding more stars here and there, till she was sure she had just the effect she wanted. She reached down to her worktop, took a pinch of sparkling sugar dust, and sprinkled it lightly over the wet icing stars. She stood back. *Now* it was perfect.

Alice looked across the shop to where her mother was packaging up biscuits for one of Paris's most exclusive hotels, a regular order for their famous pâtisserie, *Vive Comme L'Éclair.*

"It's done, *Maman,*" she said.

Madame Éclair came to look. "It's a masterpiece, as always, Alice." She gasped as she noticed the shimmering icing stars.

"Are you all finished for today, *Maman*?" Alice asked. Now that the cake was ready, it would be rather useful to have the shop to herself for a while. She had plans to make. Plans that did *not* involve her mother.

"Two gâteaux to make for tomorrow morning," said Madame Éclair, "and *then* we can have a rest."

Alice glanced at the clock and frowned. "I'm afraid I used up all the angelica, *Maman,*" she said, hoping that her mother would not check the half-full packet in the *Vive Comme L'Éclair* storeroom. "I could pop to the market..."

"The market! Certainly not," said Madame Éclair.

"I need to go to Minou's to settle our bills anyway, and they sell the finest sugared peels in Paris. Besides, we need more cream. I don't know how we get through quite so much." She raised an eyebrow meaningfully at the small grey and white cat that sat on the doorstep, its nose pressed hopefully to the glass. Alice stifled a grin. It would take at least fifteen minutes for her mother to go to Minou's and back. Twice as many if Monsieur Minou was in a talkative mood. Madame Éclair folded her apron on the counter and reached for her handbag. On her way out of the shop she reached down and tickled the cat on the top of its head.

"She'll be back soon, Casper, and I'm sure there will be something in her bag for you," Alice said to the cat. "Now, settle down. I'm busy."

The cat yawned and curled up on the step, not caring how many customers it might trip up. Alice glanced at her wristwatch and got to work. She folded and filled another icing bag, swept a damp cloth across the marble counter and, working as quickly as she could, piped an intricate plan of the rooms and staircases of Le Château de Papillon on the counter. She had spent the last two weeks practising this map and she was sure she could draw it in her sleep. She had studied it daily since she'd found it in a package left for her underneath a bench by the Arc de Triomphe. On the back of the note were Alice's instructions for her evening's mission.

These notes had begun to appear a year ago. The first was delivered to the shop, a simple puzzle in an unsigned birthday card. Then there were crosswords, ciphers and treasure hunts, which Alice solved in a flash. Alice had thought it a fun game and suspected *everyone* of being their author, even Madame Éclair with her love of mystery books. But as the notes became more serious, Alice realised that her mother had nothing to do with it. Someone was training her to be a spy and, although it would have been a surprise to most thirteen-year-olds, it was not a surprise to Alice. *"You are capable,"* the tenth note had said. *"And you know why."* From then, the notes began to direct her to parcels hidden around Paris containing presents of skeleton keys, a lockpick set and notebooks full of secret codes that she read deep into the night with a torch under her blankets. And then, four months ago, Alice had been sent on her first mission, to pass a secret note to a woman who was waiting for her by one of Paris's bridges. It had been her first real test, and she had aced it. More missions had followed: collecting parcels, intercepting notes, eavesdropping in cafés. Tonight, though, was different. Tonight was going to be her biggest mission yet.

Alice stared down at the plan. It was a perfect replica of the mayor's mansion. Success depended on her accuracy. A curve of stairs ran down into a grand lobby, beyond which lay a square labelled "*BallRm*" in iced shorthand. A second layout showed rows of rooms, with doors and windows emphasised in dashed strokes.

Marking these was important. One must always be sure of an exit. A row of dots led from a room marked "*Kitchen*", through the house and to a corridor of bedrooms. It ended with a question mark.

"Through the kitchen at seven o'clock, up the backstairs," murmured Alice, smearing the glossy dots as she followed the trail with her finger. There would be at least thirty servants in the kitchen, more on the stairs. She marked out the quickest route to the upper floors, trailing her finger through one of the doorways, round a gallery and away from the Master Bedroom. At the end of the corridor, she tapped her finger against the question mark. "And then I just have to find the right room."

She glanced at the clock on the wall. Madame Éclair would be at least another ten minutes. Alice drew from her pocket a folded note and a sealed envelope. She smoothed the note flat on the counter and read her instructions again.

Tonight we entrust you with foiling *La Renarde,* the most dangerous of France's enemies. Renarde has been smuggling microfilms packed with information that would be of great interest to our enemies. She is cunning, like the fox she is named after, but we have faith in you. Our information is that she will be at the mayor's mansion tonight, with a microfilm that she has stolen from one of our agents. That microfilm contains information about many spies working against France. We must get it back. We have seen the guest list and we suspect she will travel as Isobel Smythe. Find that microfilm and take the metro to Mairie de Montrouge. When you reach the station, and only then, open our second card.

Alice stared at the sealed envelope containing the second card. Then she picked up her icing bag once more and drew another, larger question mark on the edge of the map. "And after I track down *La Renarde,*" she said to herself, "will I finally meet *you?*" She stared at the question mark. She had been invited to deliver this microfilm in person, not leave it under a bench in a park. She was sure that meant that tonight, she was going to meet whoever had been leaving the notes.

"I think I already know who you are," she whispered. "But it can't be you. It just can't. Because the dead don't write notes."

She shook her head and dashed her hand across the question mark. She was Alice Éclair, expert pâtissière and France's youngest and keenest spy. She had no time for daydreams. She had a traitor to catch.

At five o'clock, watched in awe by the delivery boy, Alice packed her Eiffel Tower cake into a box with *Vive Comme L'Éclair* printed on the front and tied it closed. She handed it to the smart young man. His mouth had almost hit the floor when he saw what she had achieved. Alice had grinned back at him. People often underestimated what she could do. She supposed it was because she was only thirteen. Her mother stifled a laugh as she waved the young man, still doing a perfect imitation of a trout, out of the shop. The cat miaowed in annoyance as he nudged it out of the way with his foot.

Madame Éclair stuck her head out of the door. "Home," she said firmly, and the cat, knowing that there would be no more treats today, slunk off down the street. Madame Éclair closed the door, turning the sign that hung at the window from *Ouvert* to *Fermé*.

"Another triumph, Alice," she said. "What should we do with our evening, do you think?"

Alice smiled. It was time for the first part of her plan. She reached under the counter and drew out a brown paper parcel sealed with the label from her mother's favourite bookshop. Madame Éclair opened it with a squeal.

"The new Christie!" she exclaimed. "But, Alice, Monsieur Boudet was sure he would not be able to get it till next month." She paused, and bit her lip.

"Darling, would you mind if I started it this evening?"

Alice laughed, while her heart gave a mini leap of triumph. She had known her mother would not be able to resist making a start on the most sought-after mystery book of the year.

"I will be fine," she said. "I want to work on some new cake designs, so I'll be busy myself."

Two hours later, Alice slipped her bedroom window open, wincing as the latch creaked. She swung herself on to the sill and expertly shinned down the drainpipe, landing with a soft thud on the pavement below. She glanced up at her mother's window. There was always the chance that she might put her book down, look out and wonder precisely why her daughter was clambering down a drainpipe. Thankfully, the curtains remained closed. Alice ran through her plan for the night once more, just to be clear, feeling a prickle of excitement under her skin in spite of the danger.

She straightened her coat and ran off into the dusk.

At seven o'clock, Alice slipped into the kitchen of the mayor's manor house on the edge of the city, straightening the crisp white maid's hat that was perched on the back of her bobbed hair. A small army of staff was receiving orders from a stern-looking housekeeper, who was ticking items off a list in her hand. Alice could hear the whispers of one of the maids saying that "everyone who was anyone" was in the house that night, but she did not let her glance move from the housekeeper at the front of the room. She was here to blend in.

"Some of the guest rooms will need attention while our guests are at dinner," the housekeeper remarked. "*Rodin Suite* needs fresh bedding and, Marie, could you take care of the flowers in *Monet* and *Gaugin*?"

The housekeeper continued with her list and, one by one, the housemaids gave quick curtseys and left the room to do their duties. Alice attached herself to a small group of rather giggly girls and followed them out. On her way past the housekeeper, Alice flicked a glance at the paper in her hand. The name the note had told her to expect – Isobel Smythe – was not on it. She felt a flash of panic, but carried on after the girls as they moved into the passageway.

She ran the list of names through her mind once

more. *Lady Constance Hardwick, Marie Ardle, Gina Mannitoc* – of course! Clever, but not clever enough. *La Renarde* must be feeling *very* sure that no one was looking for her. Alice made her way towards the back staircase that would lead to the upper floors. It was full of footmen running up and down with drinks trays, ice buckets and plates of expensive treats. She looked straight ahead and avoided eye contact. Alice had found that no one looked at a maid so long as they gave the air of completely belonging. A moment's hesitation or an uncertain look and she might be spotted.

Squeezing effortlessly past an under-butler with a clattering champagne bucket in his hands, Alice continued towards the second floor and the guest rooms. She followed the route she had sketched out just hours earlier on the bakery's worktop, crossing a gallery and reversing her route to lead away from the main stairs, slipping into an alcove as one of the staff came walking through carrying a pair of gentleman's shoes. On the second floor, she walked briskly down one of the corridors, her eyes flicking from right to left as she took in the names of the rooms etched into shining brass plaques on the doors. At the end of the corridor, she found the one she was looking for, knocked and, hearing no answer, drew from her pocket the ring of skeleton keys that had been left under a carousel in the Tuileries Garden six months ago. She inserted one into the lock, tested it and frowned. She drew another and, after a little work, she heard the lock click open. Alice slid into the room, being careful to close the door behind her and lock it again.

"Gina Mannitoc" was not a tidy lady. Evening dresses lay strewn across her bed and her jewel case sat wide open spewing diamonds on the vanity table. She had clearly had some difficulty deciding what to wear this evening. Alice ignored all of this and made a beeline for the wardrobe, where a bundle of scarves hung from the handle of the open door and velvet shoeboxes were piled in a teetering heap. She wrenched open the first box, tutted and cast it aside. There was nothing of interest in the second or third boxes either, but in the fourth were the shoes Alice was looking for. She had a pair at home, a gift left for her under a bridge by Saint-Chapelle. They were made by a small workshop in Cannes that asked no questions and provided elegant footwear for half the spies in France.

She lifted the shoes out of the box and, with one in each hand, felt the weight of them. Discarding the left, she turned her attention to the right, feeling her way around the heel for the tiny catch that she knew would be there. Her nail caught against something on the underside of the sole and she smiled. She pressed the catch and the heel of the shoe sprang open and deposited a film canister into her palm.

"Excellent," she said, pocketing it. She slid her hand into her other pocket and withdrew an identical roll, which she slotted into the shoe, and then placed the boxes back as they had been. Alice smiled. She was getting good at this.

She moved towards the door and froze.

"I just need my shawl. I want to watch the fireworks later and it's so cold outside." The voice was nearby. Just outside the door. Alice heard the sound of the key in the lock.

She scanned the room for places to hide. The bed was too high to conceal her underneath. She would be in full view the minute the woman walked through the door. The shawl might be in the wardrobe so hiding there was out of the question. *"Think!"* Alice hissed to herself.

"I'll only be a second," the woman called to her companion, tripping lightly into the room. She crossed the floor to the wardrobe and rooted around before emerging with her shawl.

Outside, hanging from the windowsill by her fingertips, Alice listened as the woman hurried out of the room with a slam of the door. She swung herself back up to the sill, removed the ball of soft icing she had wedged beneath the window catch, and leapt back into the room.

Nobody saw her leave.

Nobody saw her make her way down the backstairs and into the kitchen.

Nobody saw her as she crept out into the night.

And if they did? *Well*, thought Alice, running down the lawn at the front of the mansion, *nobody really looks at a maid.*

CHAPTER
TWO

An hour later, Alice stood at a metro station on the outskirts of the city. The train had been warm, but a cold knot in Alice's stomach had grown tighter and tighter with each passing stop. She crossed the platform to a bench, sat down and drew from her pocket the second note. With trembling hands, she tore it open and stared at a jumble of letters.

NJJIRZRDGGHZZOHTGDOOGZKCVIOJHOZIJX
GJXFMPZYZ...

Alice smiled. She already knew this code. The notes had been left on a Thursday, the fifth day of the week, so she needed to count forwards five letters in the alphabet for every letter.

She pressed a finger against the side of the ring that she always wore on her left hand – two silver bands, each engraved with the alphabet marked out in marcasite. She lined up the two rings so that the "N" on the top band was above its partner on the lower band, then she clicked the top band forwards five times. "N" became "O", then "P", "Q", "R", and finally "S". Alice read off the rest of the letters. "S. O. O. N... *Soon...*"

"Soonwewill..."

"Soonwewillmeet..."

Alice gasped as the note was revealed. "*Soon we will meet, my Little Phantom. Ten O Clock, Rue de...*"

"Little Phantom." Alice almost dropped the note. Only one person in her life had called her Little Phantom – her Uncle Robert. Uncle Robert had taught her cryptic crosswords and simple ciphers. He had shown her how to use a Morse code cipher and played spy games with her, pretending to track down enemy agents in the middle of the Tuileries Garden. "Every spy needs a codename," he had told her, naming her the Little Phantom for her ability to hide in corners and sneak unseen through rooms. She had always suspected, always hoped, that whoever was leaving her the notes had known Uncle Robert, and here was the proof.

"Could it even *be* you?" she whispered. But that was ridiculous. Robert Éclair had drowned in the Seine two years ago, a year before the notes began to arrive. Alice missed him so dearly, with his burly frame and his laugh that started deep in his belly and erupted from his mouth in an explosion of joy.

Alice left the station and set off down one of the

wide avenues, following the directions she had been given to a dark mansion set aside from the street. When she was within a few metres of its gates, she paused and adjusted the buckle on her shoe, checking behind her to make sure no one was around. Then she slipped through the gates, headed noiselessly down the path and knocked at the door. There was no response. Alice was about to knock again when she noticed a scrap of paper hanging from the door handle. It was in code. It said: *Phantoms do not knock.*

She pushed at the door and it swung open into a hallway lit by only a hanging lantern. Down the corridor she could hear the crackling of a fire. She took a breath, stepped inside, closed the door gently behind her and crept down the corridor, taking pains not to let her feet scuff against the floor. A spy must always be careful of any invitation. It could be a trap.

In a small room at the end of the corridor, she could see the back of an armchair, and in it a man in his mid-forties sat reading. Alice felt her skin prickle. Glancing from side to side in case there should be a sudden ambush from behind the doors to her right, she slowed her steps and edged carefully into the room.

The man barely looked up from his book. He simply turned a page.

"You will have to try harder than that, Alice," he muttered. "The third floorboard in the hallway is a little creaky, and you rustled against the wallpaper while avoiding the hatstand." And then he laughed, a great belly laugh that filled the room.

Alice froze.

"I knew it was you!"

Robert Éclair stood and faced her. He looked remarkably good for someone who had been dead for two years. His hair was a little greyer than Alice remembered, but he was still a great bear of a man. Alice found that, rather than running to hug him as she had imagined she would do, the knot in her stomach had grown so large that it anchored her to the floor. She felt happy and angry all at once. Hot tears pricked at the side of her eyes, spilling their salt down her cheeks.

"But you're dead," she blurted out.

Uncle Robert laughed again. Then he stood, crossed the room and led her to one of the vast armchairs by the fire. Above the blood that was rushing through her ears, Alice heard a clattering and realised that he had placed a teacup into her shaking hands and was ladling in sugar.

"Very much not dead, Alice," he said. "There is too much work to do to waste time on death."

Alice gulped down her tea. "But you fell," she objected. "You fell into the river."

"And did they ever fish me out?"

He sat down opposite her. "I'm sorry, my dear. I wanted to let you know earlier. You are my favourite niece, after all."

"I'm your *only* niece," Alice retorted.

Uncle Robert ignored this.

"Alice, you know what my job was when I was ... alive?"

Alice nodded. They had never actually talked of this, but she had always known, really. Uncle Robert knew too much about ciphers and codes and was too good at disappearing to be anything else.

"You really *were* a spy," she said.

"Well done," said Uncle Robert. "A very *good* spy. I was trusted with many very important missions. I like to think that I passed on just a little of my skill to you in all the games we played, breaking codes in the Musée D'Orsay. Do you remember when I hid your birthday present in the middle of Montmartre and made you solve clues to find it?"

Alice nodded. Uncle Robert had been such fun to be around. Then he had gone, and there had been a great void in her life. She felt a rush of anger. How *dare* he make such light of this.

"One of my missions made it too dangerous for me to carry on," he said. "As a spy you make enemies. As a successful spy you make *lots* of them, and my masters decided that I should ... retire. So we threw a sack of flour into the river, sent a message to your mother that I had died and..." He spread his hands out to take in the warm study. Alice scanned the room, books piled high on the desk and maps sprawling across the walls. Above the mantlepiece was a map of Paris, peppered with pins and coloured thread linking one place to another, and luggage tags scribbled with code tacked into place. On some of the luggage tags there was a tiny wisp inked in blue pen. A phantom.

"Is that me?" she asked.

Uncle Robert glanced at the map and smiled.

"Yes. I'm very proud of you, Alice. I knew you had promise, and look how far you've come. You've saved lives, you know. All the information you've gathered for me has been very useful. And no one ever sees you."

"Grown-ups never notice anyone who isn't one of them," Alice grumbled. "It's very annoying of them."

Uncle Robert laughed. "Well, you see, I can't carry on working – our enemies would recognise me at once – but the work is still *out there*, and you, Little Phantom, have been very useful indeed. Spying is rather difficult when you are dead, you know."

He gave a wry smile. Alice felt the knot in her stomach tighten again. It was all very well him flattering her and telling her what a great job she had done, and she had loved all her missions, but…

"You *lied* to us!" she blurted out. "*Maman* and I have missed you so much."

"I'm sorry, Alice," Uncle Robert said, his face serious. "I would have told you, but what did the notes tell you a spy must remember above all things?"

Alice frowned. "Trust no one. But that doesn't

apply to family!"

"Even family," said Uncle Robert. "You might have revealed that you knew I was alive, or come looking for me. It was safer for you not to know. France is more important than our family. Never forget that. And speaking of our work..." He held out his hand. Alice paused for a second, but the look on her uncle's face made it clear that discussion of his two years' absence was finished. Reluctantly, she dug one hand into her coat pocket to retrieve the film canister. Uncle Robert snatched it from her palm.

"Help yourself to cake, Alice," he said, before hauling himself out of the chair and opening the door to what looked like a cupboard. At the door, he paused as if something had just occurred to him.

"One thing, Alice. Was I right about *La Renarde? Is* she travelling as Isobel Smythe?"

Alice could not help but smile. "No. You were wrong," she said, glad that she knew something he didn't. "But I worked out her pseudonym anyway."

She got up, walked over to her uncle's desk and wrote the word *GINA MANNITOC* on a slip of paper, using his beautiful jade fountain pen. She crossed out the letter 'I' and wrote it at the bottom of the paper. Then she did the same with 'A', 'M' and the rest. A grin spread over Uncle Robert's face.

"I am incognita," he said. "Clever, but not clever enough!"

"Exactly what I thought," said Alice. "Quite clumsy, really. Almost as though she wanted to be caught."

"Or thought she was under no suspicion. Remember, Alice, our best chances often occur when the enemy drops its guard." He tossed the film canister lightly between his hands and then went into the cupboard and closed the door.

Alice went to examine the map above the mantlepiece in more detail, tracing the threads that connected Paris's streets with her finger. There was a pin for the place where she had found the microfilm, and one for the park where she had picked up a parcel from beneath a bench last week. Another marked the spot near the Eiffel Tower where she had tailed a man in a blue coat while planning a design for a wedding cake. She remembered that she had almost lost sight of him while trying to decide on whether to ice filigree or flowers around the base. She looked for *Vive Comme L'Éclair* and found it marked beneath another wispy "Little Phantom" tag. To the right was a tag marked with a ring of stars and three dots in the middle. Alice peered at it. The dots might be an "s" in Morse code, but what if it was something else? She reached out a hand to see if anything was written on the back.

"Alice, come and look at this," Uncle Robert called, pushing open the cupboard door and motioning for Alice to enter. The small space was lit by a red bulb and Alice had to squint to adjust her eyes to the dim light. Along one wall was a workbench on which were sat two vats filled with chemicals. A washing line was strung from wall to wall above them, a reel of wet film hanging from it, dripping on to the stone floor. Uncle Robert handed Alice a magnifying glass and, with gloved hands, pulled the film towards her.

"Look at this one. This was taken by one of our loyal agents just two days ago and then stolen by *La Renarde*. She will stop at nothing to put us in danger. These are photos of agents we need to capture. One of them could be *La Renarde* herself." He pointed at the frame. "Look where this one is going."

Alice squinted. A dark figure in a long coat,

the hood pulled up so that there was no way of seeing their face, was entering a shop on one of Paris's streets. She read the sign above the door. "sserpxe erihppas."

"It is backwards, Alice. Have you never used a roll of film before? It's the office of the Sapphire—"

"The Sapphire Express!" exclaimed Alice. "Oh, how glamorous."

"Indeed," murmured Uncle Robert. He ran his fingers down the length of the film roll and pointed to a frame at the end. Alice squinted at it. It was a picture of a scrap of paper.

"What is that?" she asked.

"Information about the spy. Photographing notes can be a useful way of passing information. Our agent made a few gentle enquiries at the train office, wrote the information down and took a photo of his notes. It should all have gone so smoothly, then *La Renarde* stole the film."

"And I got it back," grinned Alice.

Uncle Robert sighed and let the film drop from his fingers. "With this information we could get to the heart of the operation. No wonder *La Renarde* was so keen to stop us having it. It confirms that there is one way that we can strike at them, but we could never risk it."

"Why not?"

"Because it would be impossible for me and dangerous for you. I would be recognised at once, which would be most unfortunate given that I am meant to be dead, and you... Well, even if you could make it on board, which I doubt, it would be far too dangerous."

"On board?"

"Yes," said Uncle Robert. "On the Sapphire Express."

Alice gasped. The Sapphire Express was a train to rival the famous Orient Express. Alice had heard her mother describe it as a palace driven by steam, every inch covered in beautiful panelling, intricate glasswork and gleaming gold.

Uncle Robert nodded. "Those papers you picked up for me in the Louvre last month were very cleverly coded, but I broke them eventually and they were extremely enlightening. An enemy spy is to travel south soon, carrying passports and papers that could help a dozen enemy spies disappear. British passports made for fake identities. We suspected that the spy might take one of the train routes and now, because of this film, we know." He tapped the frame of the film that showed the coded note. "It's all in here, Alice. They will be on the Sapphire Express to Marseilles this Thursday, travelling First Class and boarding at Paris."

"With the papers?" asked Alice.

He nodded. "Alice, if those papers reach Marseilles and are passed on, dozens of enemy spies will be able to pass into France and across the Channel. Our allies will be in terrible danger."

"What do we know about them?" Alice asked. "Is it *La Renarde*?"

Uncle Robert shook his head. "No, not her. We don't know much about this agent. They are as slippery as an eel, so we call them *L'Anguille*. They are an excellent codesmith, obviously. We know that they have travelled recently: to Austria, and to England. And that was just last week. Imagine! If we'd known, we could have moved on them then. Other than that, we know very little. If only there was a way for one of us to be on that train. We could identify the spy and intercept those papers."

He leaned back in his chair and looked at Alice

from out of the side of his eyes.

"It's a shame," he said, one eyebrow raised. "It might have been the perfect job for my Little Phantom."

Alice did not answer. A part of her was still furious with Uncle Robert for lying to her, but he had trusted that she would turn into a good spy and she wanted to show him how good she really could be. Her mind was working quickly and she thought she may just have a way for the Little Phantom to be on that train after all.

CHAPTER
THREE

The next afternoon, Alice sat perched on a bench watching people walk in and out of a door marked *Sapphire Express.* She was dressed in her smartest day outfit and a neat black wool jacket. A square leather case sat next to her on the bench. So did Casper, who had followed her through the city in the hope of there being something edible in the case. In the ten minutes in which Alice had waited, half a dozen people had bustled in or out of the door – serious businessmen and excited holiday-makers eager to secure a berth on the country's most luxurious train. Alice glanced at her wristwatch. Time was speeding away. She waited as a young man in a flamboyant green waistcoat with a peach handkerchief in his jacket pocket walked down the steps. He paused at the bottom to run a hand over the perfect quiff of his hair then set off towards the metro station.

"Stay there, Casper," Alice said, and she snatched her case from the bench, crossed the street and entered the navy-blue door of the Sapphire Express bureau.

"We ask that all bookings be made by a parent or guardian," the woman behind the desk said, motioning for Alice to sit in the plush velvet chair opposite. From the walnut panelling inlaid with delicate flower motifs, to the settees upholstered in petrol-blue velvet, the offices of the Sapphire Express were designed to show off the glamour and comfort of the train itself.

"Will your mother or father be joining you?" the woman continued, reaching for a small bell which would doubtless summon a pot of coffee to smooth any negotiations over the price of a berth on the train in high season.

Alice shook her head. "I'm not here to make a booking," she said. "I'm a pastry chef."

The woman's bright smile faded and the bell was replaced on the desk.

"We are not hiring any more staff this season," she said crisply. "We are at full capacity on all trains. I'm sorry you have had a wasted journey."

Alice had known that there would not be a job available for her to just walk into, and she had prepared for this. She just had to hold her nerve. *Maman* always said to "remember your greatest triumph when facing your greatest challenge", so she pictured the Eiffel Tower with its spun-sugar fireworks and found that her voice rang clear and confident in the small office as she said, "I think you will want to hire me."

The woman looked her up and down and let out a snort. "I assure you, my dear, we have all the pastry chefs we need. *Trained* ones."

Alice unclipped her case and placed it on the table. The four sides fell away, revealing a perfect replica of the train created from sugar biscuit and glossy icing. The windows were made from spun sugar, edible gold leaf picking out the lanterns and the insignia on the side of each carriage. Alice leaned forwards and touched one of the wheels, making it turn on its biscuit-work spindle.

The woman's eyes widened. She leaned forwards to examine the inside of the carriage, where Alice had recreated the train's panelling and flock wallpaper in glossy icing and careful texture work. Plain biscuit passengers sat at each table, enjoying tiny glasses of champagne, each rendered in crisp sugar.

"You didn't have time to decorate the passengers, I see," the woman said archly.

Alice smiled. This was just what she was hoping

the woman would say.

"I didn't know who they would be before this morning," she replied and, being sure not to damage any of the delicate interior of the carriage, she took the six passengers and arranged them in front of her. She drew a set of nozzles and icing bags from a pouch in her case and worked quickly on each passenger, filling in clothing, hair and faces till the six people who had left the office that morning sat in front of her. Every detail was perfect. The shining shoes of the nervous-looking woman and her husband with the florid complexion. The slick quiff of the young man in the green waistcoat with the peach pocket square. Alice had even picked out the scar on the cheek of the businessman with the heavy beard and bitten nails.

"I think that is everyone," she smiled, returning the passengers to the carriage.

The look on the woman's face told Alice she was hired.

"*Monte Carlo?*" Madame Éclair gasped.

Alice bit her lip. Convincing the woman at the Sapphire Express to take on an additional pastry chef was one thing. Persuading her mother to let her travel to the South of France on her own, and at such short notice, was quite another.

"It's such an opportunity," she said. "Just think, *Maman*, a chance to try out my pâtisserie skills on the very highest members of society."

Madame Éclair looked around the shop with despair. "But how are we to cope without you, Alice? There are orders to be fulfilled."

Alice shook out her apron and tied it round her waist. "Then I will just have to get to work on them now. I'll only be away for three days, *Maman*. And one of those is Sunday. And when I come back, you will be able to tell our customers that we have a pastry chef who has worked on the *Sapphire Express* itself!"

Madame Éclair's lips went very thin. "How did this opportunity arise, Alice?" she asked sternly.

"I just went to enquire whether they would consider taking our pastries," Alice said, smiling. "They won't, but they said they were short of a pastry chef for the next trip to the South and would I consider a short contract to demonstrate what we could offer."

What the woman had *actually* said was that they would take Alice on a trial run. She was to produce pastries as ingenious as her iced train to impress the passengers, whom she had been assured had *extremely* high standards. Alice's heart raced as she remembered the woman's parting words to her. "If you can earn your keep, there may be a job for you. If not, our *maître d'* will put you off the train. I'm sure a resourceful young woman like you should have no difficulties making your own way home."

"I promise I will be back by Tuesday," Alice urged. "And I can tell you all about the train, and *Vive Comme L'Éclair* will be the talk of France's richest set!"

Madame Éclair shrugged her shoulders. "How can I refuse that?" she admitted. "Promise you will take good care of yourself. Thirteen is young to go away for the first time, Alice. Stay out of any trouble."

It was a statement, not a question, and Alice was glad she did not have to answer. It was not a promise she could have made.

CHAPTER
FOUR

Alice had been told to report to the concierge at Paris Nord at two o'clock sharp to be given her uniform and orders for the day's work. She had been delayed by Casper whining for treats as she had left the shop, finally resorting to bribing him with a dish of cream so that she could escape. The minute hand was ticking close to the hour as she walked towards the entrance, the great glass arch of the station front rising above her, glinting in the sunlight. Alice felt her grip tighten on her small case as she walked under the watchful eye of the statues that ran along the top of the entrance and into the station's bustling halls, but she lifted her chin high and smiled at the sharp click of her heels against the gleaming floor.

For the first time, she began to feel like one of the glamorous agents that Uncle Robert had told her about. Maybe in her next mission she could take the part of a society lady. She lifted one hand to slick a lock of hair behind her ear, as she had seen the beautiful guests at the mansion do, and pulled her mouth into a little pout, tilting her head to one side and hoping that she looked as sophisticated as she imagined.

"Oof!"

Alice fell forwards. Her case flew from her grasp and skidded across the floor to thud against the side of a ticket desk. The lock failed and the case burst open, scattering its contents across the floor. Alice hit the ground with a hard thump, wincing as her knees scuffed across the tiles. All the air was pushed out of her lungs with a sharp *whump*.

"Oh my! What have I done?" a cultured voice called out in English.

Alice struggled to her feet, gasping as she tried to catch her breath. She became vaguely aware of a teenage girl beside her, ineffectively swiping at her jacket with a wisp of a lace handkerchief.

"I'm so very, very sorry. I just wasn't watching where I was going. Papa has gone to get our tickets and a horrid little man came up to talk to me and I just wanted to get away from him, and I couldn't see Papa, and, well, I wasn't watching where I was going. Oh, I've said that, haven't I?"

Alice, still smarting from the fall, was hardly listening to the torrent of words. From the corner of her eye, she could see passengers stepping over her case, not seeming to mind that they were kicking her notebooks across the dusty floor.

Her notebooks! Her codes. Her ciphers. Her cake designs.

"Oh, no!" she cried.

She dashed across the station floor, buffeted by people hurrying for their trains and almost tripping over the long leash of a snarling Pekinese that snapped at her ankles as she fled past. Reaching her case, she dropped to her knees and scrabbled to cram everything back inside. She rescued her dictionary from under a woman's high-heeled shoe and frowned to see that the cover had torn away from the spine. She gathered up her notebooks, carefully counting them to make sure none were missing.

"The blue one. The blue one," she muttered in alarm, looking around wildly. It was her most precious code book. Oh *why* hadn't she tucked it safely away in a pocket?

"Do you mean that one over there?"

Alice looked up. The girl with the handkerchief had followed her across the station. She looked a little older than Alice, perhaps fifteen or sixteen, and she was dressed exquisitely in a pink day dress with matching cashmere jacket. Her glossy blonde hair was perfectly bobbed with a delicate wave and she wore what Alice's mother would have called "almost make-up" – a dash of rouge and a light lipgloss. She was pointing to a book lying open by a woman in a wheelchair in the middle of the station.

"Don't worry, I'll get it." And before Alice could stop her, she strode over to pick the book up.

"No, I'll go..." started Alice, slamming her case shut and staggering to her feet, but the young woman had already reached the notebook and was bending down to pick it up. Alice bounded forwards as the young woman tripped across to her, holding out the book.

"Is that what they call shorthand?" she asked brightly, nodding towards the ciphers set out in Morse code on the open page. "Such funny scribbles."

Alice flushed. "Yes," she lied. "A girl can never have too many skills, as my mother says."

The young woman turned the book upside down and squinted at it. "Must be awfully useful for disguising one's diary. Perhaps we should all learn."

Trying not to snatch, Alice took the book from the

girl's hand and flicked through it, checking that none of the precious pages had been lost. She sighed with relief and slipped it into her jacket pocket, taking care to button it carefully.

The girl laughed. "I don't have any at all. Skills, that is, not diaries. I have *heaps* of diaries. My papa thinks quite the opposite to your mama. We're not meant to have skills, you know. We're meant to have *accomplishments.* That's why I'm going to Nice. I'm being sent to finishing school to learn to be a young lady."

Alice stared at her. The girl in front of her was every inch a young lady already. Alice dared not glance over at the shining glass of the station's windows in case she caught sight of herself. She knew that next to such a groomed vision she would look like a total ragamuffin. And, oh, how she had wanted to appear sophisticated.

"My goodness, my manners!" the girl exclaimed. "No wonder Papa is keen to get me into school." She presented her hand with a swift, gracious movement. "Penelope Fulmington, of the Berkshire Fulmingtons, England," she said.

Alice took Penelope's hand, hoping that her own

was not too dirty. "Alice Éclair," she said. "From … um … Paris."

"How divine!" Penelope said. "I've just loved being in Paris. Papa let us stay for two days. I've seen your beautiful tower and, oh, ever so many galleries. Which train are you getting? Do say it's the Sapphire Express. We can sit together and you can tell me all about how wonderful it is to live in such a beautiful city."

In spite of how badly the day was going, Alice could not help but smile at the thought that Penelope could mistake her for one of the Sapphire Express's passengers.

"I'm on the Sapphire Express," she admitted. "But I'm—"

"How wonderful!" cried Penelope. "Are you booked in yet?"

"No," began Alice. "I—"

"Oh, we must sort that out and then we can go and enjoy tea until it's time to board," cried Penelope, and, without listening to Alice's alarmed protests, she grasped her by the elbow and began steering her towards the office of the Sapphire Express.

The man behind the desk leafed through paperwork, looking for Alice's name.

"Your name is not here, Mam'selle. Are you sure that your journey is today?"

Alice blushed a deep pink and shot an apologetic look at Penelope.

"There has been some mistake," she said. "I'll be under … staff."

The man raised an eyebrow and turned to a separate list.

"Mam'selle Éclair, you say… Ah yes, here… You are late, Mam'selle," he snapped, drawing a silver watch from his pocket and squinting at it. "All staff were to be on board ten minutes ago."

"There was an accident," Alice explained.

The man looked her up and down, taking in her dusty dress and scuffed knees. "So I can see. You can change on board and then get straight to your post. And you, Mam'selle…" The man's voice faltered as he noticed the elegant cut of Penelope's clothes. He rose to his feet, his hands clasped in front of him. "I beg your pardon, Mam'selle, I assumed that you were…"

"Together?" asked Penelope evenly. "Indeed, we

are. Mam'selle Éclair helped me out when a ruffian attempted to steal my purse – and I do not like your tone."

Alice gasped. She was not sure what shocked her most – that this well-to-do girl would lie so brazenly or that she would do so to help a stranger who had turned out to be "staff". The man glanced down at the desk and Penelope winked at Alice.

"I trust that Mam'selle Éclair will not be inconvenienced for coming to my aid," she said, her face once again stern.

The man mumbled an apology and, with a grimace that did not escape Alice, motioned towards a door marked *Privée*.

"The platform is that way, Mam'selle Éclair. Ask for Monsieur Armand and he will show you to your cabin. I will attend to Mam'selle..."

"Fulmington," provided Penelope. She held out a hand to Alice. "Goodbye, Alice, see you on board. And thank you again for rescuing my purse from that absolute *beast* of a man." She leaned forwards and whispered, "I'm so glad someone my own age will be on board. It will be much more fun to chat to you than to some of the stuffy people Papa will want me to talk with."

Alice smiled, but her uncle's warning of "trust no one" rang in her head. It was silly to think that Penelope could be a spy, but then, no one would suspect Alice either. Besides, she was sure that, once on board, any friendship with Penelope would be firmly discouraged.

This was confirmed a moment later. "Mam'selle Éclair..." the man at the desk said pointedly, getting up to open the door to the platform. The scent of coal smoke drifted through, making Alice's nose prickle, and she saw Penelope lift her hand to her face and give a genteel cough. The man leaned close to Alice's ear and hissed, his voice not quite drowned out by the noise from the platform, "You will be expected to keep to your own class while in our employment, Mam'selle. Do not forget your place unless you wish to lose it."

Alice nodded and stepped through the doorway. The man cast one final meaningful glare in her direction and then the door closed on him, and Alice turned to take a look at the Sapphire Express.

CHAPTER
FIVE

The train was part fire dragon, part shimmering beetle. The sapphire-blue engine belched smoke and gleaming coaches with paintwork polished to a mirrored shine stretched down the platform.

Stewards hurried past Alice, pushing luggage trolleys piled high with monogrammed cases and trunks. A harried maid dashed by, dabbing with a cloth at the collar of an embroidered cloak. Alice tugged at the hem of her jacket and set off for the carriage halfway down the platform where liveried staff darted in and out, their arms laden with pressed linen and boxes stamped with the mark of Paris's most exclusive shops. This was the hub of the train, between the luxury of the First Class sleeping carriages and the more ordinary accommodation provided to Third Class ticket holders. It was where Alice would be spending the next three days as the train travelled to Monte Carlo and back.

Alice picked up her pace, eager to be on board. As she reached the steps, a frazzled-looking boy with a pile of starched towels almost taller than himself pushed past her, the rim of his hat slipping over his eyes. Alice straightened his hat as he went by and he turned to flash her a look of thanks.

"Linen cupboard six," snapped a short man in a petrol-blue waistcoat. "Back here, sharpish. Butter knives arriving from the silversmith's." The man looked over the rim of his spectacles at Alice and raised an eyebrow. "Third Class is down the platform, Mam'selle."

Alice swept a hand over her skirt, suddenly reminded that she must still look so dusty. "My name is Alice Éclair," she explained. "'I'm the new pâtissière."

The man's bland expression barely flickered. "Pastry cook. Éclair. You're late. Staff cabin 4d. Top berth. Caron will show you." He flicked a finger towards a nervous-looking girl about Alice's age. "Don't take too long getting into your uniform," the man warned. "Chef will be wanting you."

He waved a hand down the train and turned to bark more orders at a trio of maids. The girl called Caron shot Alice a half-smile and dashed into the train. Alice did not have time to ask Caron what her first name was. Instead, she followed her as she sprang up the steps and hurried down a narrow corridor to a row of cabins.

"This is ours." Caron threw open the door of a tiny

cabin for two. Alice peered in and her heart sank. She had known that she would not be travelling in luxury, but the room was barely bigger than a cupboard. There were bunk beds along one wall, each with a navy-blue blanket and a rather thin-looking pillow. A small sink was squeezed into the corner below the cabin window and there was a bare clothes rail on which hung a smart white chef's jacket and navy dress.

"That's for you," Caron said, and before Alice could thank her, the cabin door clicked shut and she was gone.

Alice settled her case on the luggage rack next to the sink and reached up to take the uniform from its hanger. She struggled with the buttons a little and realised that her fingers were trembling. It had been exciting to get on board, but the challenge ahead was suddenly real. She had to make sure she stayed on board for at least long enough to unmask the spy. She drew from her pocket her notebook with sketches for pastries that she had planned to make to impress the *maître d'*. Somehow they seemed amateurish and simple now. How could she keep up with the demands of the *maître d'* while spotting the spy? What if she was thrown off before they had even circled Paris?

She heard her mother's voice at the back of her head. "It's all about timing and keeping your pans boiling," Madame Éclair would say while Alice tried to whip up several different caramels at once.

"You can do this," Alice said out loud, and she unbuttoned the collar of the dress. She changed quickly and rearranged her hair, tying her fringe away from her face with a fresh ribbon, and made her way back to the kitchen. The *maître d'* was midway through a torrent of instructions to four men in chef uniforms.

"...and after the filet of beef they will have *crème au chocolat,*" he said, closing the small leather notebook in his hand and slipping it into a waistcoat pocket.

"Ah, Mam'selle Éclair," he said. "The young lady who had such a surprising effect on Madame Picot at the office. Your reputation precedes you. I thought we would start with *petits fours* to accompany coffee. Something to rival the work that you showed Madame Picot should suffice."

"I had planned salted caramel macarons for

coffee," said one of the chefs, glaring at Alice. " No one informed me that Mam'selle Éclair was joining us. What is the use of *two* chefs working on desserts? Do you have no need for me now? Would Mam'selle Éclair like to turn her hand to *crème au chocolat* or am I still trusted with that?"

The *maître d'* smiled at him. "Chef Albert, your desserts are renowned from here to Marseilles. No one can create a *crème au chocolat* to rival yours. The company merely thought Mam'selle Éclair could offer additional treats. Biscuits, small things to melt away in an instant. Not the centrepieces that we rely upon you for."

"And where do I find space for her?" Chef Albert looked a little mollified, but it was still clear that Alice was not entirely welcome in the kitchen. She gulped. Another hurdle, as if she didn't have enough already. She glanced round the small galley kitchen. Every inch of the walls was crammed with box-shelves, tiny drawers and utensils securely fixed with clips. The counter space was carefully marked out, with the tools of each chef set out in pots fixed to the counters. She wasn't sure where she could fit. Then she spotted a small, awkwardly shaped space near the serving hatch. It was out of the way of the other chefs, but she could watch staff coming and going in the corridor outside. It was perfect.

"I could squeeze myself in there if no one else is using it," she suggested.

"Excellent," said the *maître d'*. "That is solved." Chef Albert looked as though he had something else to add, but thought better of it.

The *maître d'* looked at Alice. "Welcome on board, Mam'selle Éclair, but I want to inspect everything you create before it leaves the galley. We have the very highest standards in France to uphold."

"He's less fierce than he seems," the head chef said to Alice as the *maître d'* left the kitchen. "But understand this, all of you. Everything that leaves this kitchen must demonstrate the perfection that is the hallmark of the Sapphire Express. Now, let's start." He took a watch out of his waistcoat pocket and frowned. "The passengers board in two hours and we should greet them with afternoon coffee. Mam'selle Éclair, your first chance to impress us with..." He caught Chef Albert's glance. "What do you think, Albert?"

Albert smiled. "*Mille-feuille*, I think."

Alice felt a knot of worry form in the pit of her stomach. Of all the pastries she was asked to make at *Vive Comme L'Éclair, mille-feuille* was the one that most often left her crying with frustration at unrisen puff pastry or burned edges. And the pastry alone could take two hours to prepare. Albert turned to his own counter and began whistling as he took down the ingredients to make his chocolate ganache for later. He had done this on purpose, she was sure of it. Was she going to fail and be thrown off board even before she had had a chance to take a look at the passengers?

"Mam'selle Éclair?" asked the head chef.

Alice swallowed the small knot of worry down. She *had* to get this right.

"Yes, Chef," she said.

Two hours later, Alice was crouched on the floor of the kitchen, glancing nervously between her wristwatch and the oven door. The passengers had started to gather on the platform and she had spent the last half-hour bobbing in and out of the galley kitchen to try to take a sneak peek at them as they entered the train. But every time she left the oven it would draw her back with a suspicious whiff of smoke or a crackle that warned of puff pastry singed at the edges. At home she could separate out her spying from her work in the pâtisserie, but here that would be impossible. How was she ever going to even get a glimpse of the passengers if she could not leave the kitchen? To think that all that stood between her and the saving of France was a burned pastry or a curdled custard!

She glared at the puff pastry through the oven door. Should she take a peek or leave it just one more minute? Behind her she could hear Jacques, one of the *chef de partie*, grinding coffee beans as he hummed a song to himself. Jacques' counter spot was by one of the galley's small windows, looking out on to the platform. It would be the perfect place from which to watch the passengers arriving. Alice reached for a small bowl, some vanilla extract and a tub of cream.

Ten minutes later, she had a perfect bowl of whipped vanilla cream in front of her. She had added in just the merest touch of nutmeg to give it warmth, and then folded it into soft peaks. She breathed in its rich sweetness and then carried it over to Jacques.

"Could you taste this for me, please? I want to make sure it is absolutely perfect. I thought it would go nicely with the *mille-feuille.*"

Jacques picked up a tasting spoon from his own counter and scooped a portion of cream. Alice saw his eyes widen and knew that her vanilla cream would pass the taste test of the Sapphire Express kitchen.

"I think I'll just try another spoonful," said Jacques. Alice grinned and took the opportunity to glance out of the window. She saw Penelope dashing past, dragging an older man who must be her father behind her and talking at double speed. Then a slightly stooping elderly man, clutching a book in one hand and a rather battered suitcase in the other.

"It's absolutely delicious!" said Jacques, dragging Alice's attention back to the kitchen.

She smiled at him. "I'm so glad," she began. "The *maître d'* seemed—"

There was a crash and a shrill cry outside. Jacques and Alice almost bashed their heads together trying to look out of the small window.

Outside on the platform were three of the Sapphire Express's passengers. One of them, a red-headed woman in a jade coat, had fallen to the floor and was being helped up by one of two young men dressed in matching dove-grey suits.

"I do apologise, miss," said one of the young men in a low drawl, taking his hat off and holding it apologetically in front of him.

"Irving never looks where he is going," said his companion.

"Americans," muttered Jacques. "Jake and Irving Hopper. I hear they are dancers of some sort. They're with us all the way to Monte Carlo. That woman must be the passenger in compartment three. She's the only woman in First Class travelling alone and she's getting off at Nice. Probably going to spend all summer sunning herself on the beach while the rest of us work."

Alice peered at the three passengers, trying to spot any clue that one of them could be *L'Anguille*. But each seemed as likely, or unlikely, as the other. Could the red-headed woman be hiding microfilms in that smart handbag that she was holding so closely to her side? Could the young men be working together? Perhaps it had not been an accident that they had bumped into her? But they were clearly travelling as a pair and Uncle Robert had not mentioned that *L'Anguille* had an accomplice.

Alice sneaked a glance back at the oven and decided to risk investigating further. She left Jacques gawping at the small group through the window and crept out of the kitchen and into the narrow corridor that ran the length of the carriage. On the way out of the door, she picked up a small pallet of glossy eggs that was on the end of the counter. Staff were always less conspicuous if they looked like they had a job to do.

She swung open the door to the platform and stepped out with the air of someone who has to be somewhere. The young men and the elegant woman were just ahead of her and, as she reached their group, she slowed a little and adjusted her grip on the pallet. Her thumb smeared the not-quite-dry ink of a stamp on the white wood and Alice tutted and moved her thumb, revealing the name of a farm and a sketch of a map of the outskirts of Avignon. Something about it seemed familiar. Where had Alice seen this before? Of course, it was at Minou's. The farm was one of their suppliers, some of the finest eggs in France.

"Didn't I see you at Le Touquet this year?" the woman was saying.

Was Alice imagining it, or did a look pass between the two men?

"Not us, ma'am," one of them replied. "Irving and I have been busy with our tour. Not got time for sunning ourselves on the beach."

"How strange," murmured the woman. "In my job it pays to be observant, and you both seem so familiar."

Jake coughed and, taking the woman's arm, steered her away from the platform edge. "Careful there, ma'am," he said. "You don't want to get dirt over those swell shoes now."

Irving had started to talk about all the places they had been in Paris and soon the trio were boarding the train at the next carriage, where the *maître d'* was waiting to greet them. Alice held back just long enough to see them disappear into the train, Irving still chattering away so that the woman could not get a word in. Then she turned on her heel and headed back towards the kitchen.

Jake had definitely not wanted to talk about Le Touquet, she thought, looking keenly at the well-swept platform. That fuss about the woman's shoes had just been a ruse to change the subject. The two men were hiding something. It was not much of a lead, but it was a start.

Alice was almost at the door to the kitchen carriage when the scent of burned butter made her nose twitch. With a cry of "Oh no!" she threw herself up the steps into the carriage and dashed to the oven, where telltale plumes of smoke were stealing into the room.

Alice dropped the egg pallet on to the counter, grabbed a teacloth and wrenched open the oven door. She gasped as the heat and smoke hit her full in the face, wafted it aside and reached in to rescue what was left of the puff pastry squares. Each and every one of them was singed around the edges, the pastry curling off the tray, brittle and cracking. Alice's heart sank. Her first test as a pastry chef on board and she had failed. There was not enough time to remake the pastry and the *mille-feuille* were utterly ruined.

"*The worst disaster is food for the birds,*" said

a voice at the back of her head. It was Madame Éclair's favourite saying, passed down from Alice's grandmama. It meant that nothing was ever truly wasted. Madame Éclair had first used it when Alice's buttermilk cake failed to rise, so she turned it into a delicious biscuit base for a peach tart. She used it when her biscuits crumbled and she whipped them into a cream concoction with fresh berries. Everything from burned edges to runny icing could be used for *something* in *Vive Comme L'Éclair*. Alice was not about to give the *maître d'* an excuse to put her off the train before it had even pulled out of the station. She reached for a knife and got to work.

CHAPTER
SIX

"Mam'selle Éclair, I have never seen anything quite like it," Henri the head chef remarked, looking in frank admiration at the plate in front of him. Alice had cut circles from the centres of the puff pastry squares, salvaging the pastry that was still perfectly puffed and almond coloured and turning them into the great wheels of the Sapphire Express. The top of each round was decorated with art nouveau icing swirls that looked just a *little* like the train's logo. Alice was particularly proud of the way that she had piped the filling between each layer of pastry to look like wisps of smoke from the train's engine. It was the sort of detail that would, doubtless, be lost on the passengers, but at least they would enjoy the buttery lightness of her pastries. Now that the burned edges had been cut away, they would melt in the mouth, she was sure of it.

"I expected something larger, but these are exquisite. I would not be ashamed to serve these in my restaurant back in Nice, Mam'selle. I hear that tiny morsels are quite the rage in Paris and the Sapphire Express is always keen to follow the latest fashions."

Alice gave an inward sigh of relief. She had passed

the first test, anyway. Her pastries were good enough to enter the Sapphire Express's dining car. The problem was getting in there *herself*. The train had a small army of white-gloved stewards who collected the coffee and dainty sandwich snacks from the kitchen on gleaming silver trays and delivered them to the dining car or to private cabins. The kitchen staff were invisible except on rare occasions when a customer wished to pass their compliments to the chef, at which point Henri would change into a pristine apron kept hung behind the kitchen door and would venture forth to graciously receive the admiration on behalf of the staff. While the layers of puff pastry had been chilling in the fridge, Alice had crept out to peer through the door of the dining car, but each time she had been sent back to the kitchen by one of the keen-eyed stewards. It was hopeless.

"Hand them to Caron," the chef said. "It's almost a shame for such works of art to be eaten, but that's what they are here for, after all."

Indeed, Alice thought. *But what I'm here for is to find a spy and I'm not going to get much chance stuck in here.*

She looked at the girl called Caron, who was waiting by the hatch into the corridor for the *mille-feuille* to be passed to her, and had an idea. She was not proud of it, but there were important things at stake here, so, as Alice passed the plate across to Caron, she moved her hand slightly so that it just nudged a pot of strawberry jus.

"Watch out!" Caron cried. She jumped backwards too late to prevent the crimson sauce staining the front of her crisp white shirt. Alice feigned a look of horror.

"The plate caught it," she said. "I'm so sorry!"

Henri groaned. "Well, you can't go into the dining room like that," he said. "Go and change at once." He turned to Alice. "Remove that apron and smarten yourself up as quickly as you can, Mam'selle Éclair. You will have to serve the pastries yourself."

Alice's face registered utter surprise, but inside she was thinking one thing. *I did it!*

With her hair smoothed back and a clean apron on, Alice stepped out into the corridor with the pastries. As she did so there was an ear-splitting shriek of a whistle and billows of steam surrounded the train, the heat of it clinging to the windows and the scent of smoke filling the air. With a screech of metal against metal, the train gave a great lurch forwards, shuddered, then began to pull slowly out of the station.

The Sapphire Express was on its way.

Alice reached out a hand to steady herself as the train bumped forwards. As it cleared the end of the platform, it began to pick up speed and the movements became a more regular rolling, rhythmic sway that rocked the train from side to side. Alice took a step forwards and sucked in her breath as the tray tipped forwards, threatening to pitch her precious pastries to the floor.

"A duck, Mam'selle," said one of the stewards close behind her. "If you walk like a duck, you will not fall." He squeezed past her and waddled the length of the carriage with his feet spread broad and flat. It was not a walk that suited the elegance of the surroundings, but the coffee pot on the steward's tray remained upright. Alice pulled her shoulders back, lifted her tray till it was level with her eyes as she had seen the steward do, and followed him to the dining car. The steward who guarded the entrance looked her up and down, nodded and pulled back the lacquered door to admit her. *Maman* had been right. The kitchen and staff compartments might be plain, but the guest carriages on the Sapphire Express were the most luxurious rooms that Alice had ever seen. The walls of the dining carriage were covered in glossy walnut panelling, with ferns and flowers picked out in silver and mother-of-pearl. Blue velvet curtains hung at each window, pulled back with tasselled satin cord. At the tables, set with pristine starched linen and silver tableware, the guests sat in plump-cushioned chairs upholstered in velvet.

Alice glanced round the carriage at the guests. Any one of them could be *L'Anguille* and she must not miss a single clue. Penelope was sat at a table for four at the far end, opposite the man who Alice presumed must be her father. He was sitting upright with his back as stiff as if it were against a wall instead of one of the Sapphire Express's comfortable chairs. Across the aisle from them sat the woman with red hair. She was applying crimson lipstick with great aplomb, staring at herself in a hand mirror and talking loudly to Penelope's father, who appeared to be trying very hard not to make eye contact.

Penelope leaned towards her, the expression on her face one of frank admiration.

In the centre of the carriage, the older man Alice had seen from the kitchen had taken an entire table to himself. All of the Sapphire Express's beautiful plates and glassware were piled up on one corner, the gleaming silver fish knives and soup spoons half hanging off the edge. In their place he had placed book upon book. Some lay face down, their spines creaking at the indignity. Others were wide open, the man scanning one before going to another, making quick, scribbled notes on a huge ledger propped open on his knees. Alice winced as a globule of ink dripped from the man's pen on to the white table linen. She moved towards him with her tray and her hand nudged against a red leather-bound book by the man's elbow. He cried out and snatched it to his chest, running a finger protectively over the binding, then recollected himself and smiled at Alice. "So sorry, my dear," he muttered. "My books are precious, you understand."

Alice smiled an apology and placed a plate on the only spare space left on the table, squeezing it between a pile of notebooks and an open ink pot.

She paused, hoping to catch a glimpse of what was in one of the open books, but the man's arm covered them so that she could not read any part of their contents.

"I hope those are to go with the coffee," said one of the American men who Alice had seen from the galley window. He was sat at a table for two across from his companion, who turned his head to greet Alice. They were both slim and tall with confident, easy smiles that lit up their faces.

"Irving has the most appalling sweet tooth," the other man said apologetically. "I've tried so hard to cure him of it, but he would rather listen to his appetite than to his twin, it seems."

"I hope you enjoy, sir," said Alice, placing one of the dessert plates by the steaming cup of black coffee in front of him. Irving picked up a dainty pastry fork, twirled it round his fingers like a baton and dug in enthusiastically.

"Jake, you *have* to try this!" he said, loud enough for Penelope's father to turn his head and frown. "No one makes desserts like the French, huh?" He winked at Alice and she smiled back and placed a dessert in front of his twin.

"Irving and I love France, miss. We were born and bred in New Orleans, so we were brought up half-French, half-American."

"And what brought you to France? Was it just our desserts?" asked Alice.

Across the aisle she heard Penelope's father bristle. "Staff ask the most impertinent questions nowadays," he snapped.

"Nonsense," cried the red-headed woman. "Talking about ourselves is an excellent idea. After all, we should get to know one another a bit. These trips can be dreadfully dull if everyone sits in silence and there's no good gossip." She clicked her compact shut and looked rather pointedly at Alice, who nodded politely at Irving and Jake and moved down the carriage to place a plate in front of the woman.

Penelope's father pulled himself even more upright than before, though Alice did not know how that was possible. "I hardly think it is necessary for us to pry into one another's lives," he muttered.

Alice caught Penelope's eye as she served them their plates. The girl gave a little shrug and grinned at her.

"Don't be silly, Papa," she said. "It's a lovely idea." She smiled broadly at the red-headed woman. "I'm Penelope. I'm sixteen, so I'm off to Nice to be finished."

The woman laughed. "*Finishing* school? I think that would be the end of me, not the finishing." She leaned across the aisle, holding out her hand, "Stella Blyth. Journalist. Not quite finished yet."

"A journalist, huh? We could have done with a few more members of the press this last week," Irving said. "We've just finished a tour of Europe. Great audiences but not a sniff of a write-up in any of the papers."

"You're musicians?" asked Stella.

"Singers and dancers," Irving said. "Jake and Irving Hopper. The best jazz outside of New Orleans. We've done Paris, Lisbon, Copenhagen..."

Alice repeated the names in her head, listening out for names from Austria and England, where *L'Anguille* had been, but she did not hear any.

"You forgot Salzburg," objected Jake. "How could you, with its heavenly hot chocolates?"

Ah, they had been in Austria, at least, thought Alice.

"Ever been to London?" asked Stella. "We rather like a bit of jazz in Blighty!"

So Stella was English. Alice had thought so from her accent. She tucked that information away at the back of her mind. Jake nodded. "Great place. Didn't much like the food, though."

"Oh, how lovely to travel so much," Penelope sighed. "I suppose it's very glamorous. I wish I could dance."

"Now, I won't have a young lady saying she can't dance," said Jake, throwing down his napkin and winking at Irving. He sprang out of his seat and held out a hand to Penelope. She stood up and Jake spun her into his arms, and in a second they were sashaying round the carriage, Penelope squealing with delight and Irving clapping his hands and singing something lively that Alice did not recognise. Stella let out a great guffaw of laughter and winked at Mr Fulmington, who looked like he was about to explode.

As Jake whirled Penelope under his arm in the middle of the carriage, Mr Fulmington sprang to his feet and slammed his hands down on the table so hard that one of the porcelain cups bounced.

Without thinking, Alice stuck out a hand and caught it, hearing the *maître d'* puff out a breath of relief behind her.

"PENELOPE! SIT DOWN THIS MINUTE!" Mr Fulmington roared.

Penelope whipped her head round to look at her father. She lost her footing and tripped. Jake made a grasp for her hand but it was too late and, as the train rattled over a bump in the rails and made a sudden lurch, she fell backwards towards one of the stewards who had come into the carriage bearing another pot of steaming hot coffee.

Alice was suddenly aware of everything happening at once. The *maître d's* cry of alarm, Stella half rising to her feet, the words dying in Mr Fulmington's throat as he saw Penelope staggering back towards the piping-hot liquid. Alice sprang forwards, pushing Jake to one side so that he fell against the table of the elderly man and his books. She grabbed at Penelope's arm. With all the strength she could muster, she pulled the girl back towards her, spinning her away from danger.

Penelope fell into Jake's empty seat and burst into tears. Alice caught her breath and felt her knees begin to shake. She looked up at the *maître d'* who snapped his fingers at one of the stewards to attend to Penelope and then, nodding at the other passengers, strode down the carriage towards Alice.

"A word, please, Mam'selle Éclair," he said.

CHAPTER SEVEN

"But it was *my* job," complained Caron, glaring at Henri.

"The *maître d'* decides who works where on the train," said Henri calmly. "And Mam'selle Éclair's quick thinking may well have saved the Sapphire Express from an expensive lawsuit. The *maître d'* would like *her* to serve her pastries for the remainder of the trip. We will still need you to help with table clearing, obviously."

Caron bit her lip and Alice thought that the girl was trying not to cry in front of Henri. Alice felt a little bad for her, but she was also thinking of all the eavesdropping she would be able to do. Perhaps there might be a way to make it up to Caron. She waited until Henri had turned to give one of the *sous chefs* his instruction for dinner before leaning over to talk to the girl.

"I'm sorry," she whispered. "I didn't mean to."

"If you hadn't spilled that sauce..." Caron said.

Alice grimaced. That *had* been rather mean.

"I really am sorry..." She paused. "I don't know your name – your *first* name?"

"Félicité," she replied.

"I'm Alice. And I'm sorry I took your place in the

dining room."

Félicité sighed. "It's silly, really. I just wanted to see all their pretty clothes. I'm one of seven, you see, and the only girl, so all my hand-me-downs were old trousers from my brothers." She held out her starched uniform. "This is actually the nicest thing I've ever worn. I never get to spend time in smart places, and now I'm going to be stuck in the kitchen all the time."

"It won't be your only chance, I'm sure," Alice said. "We'll think of a way to get you into the dining room before the end of the trip."

Félicité smiled. "Well, it would be nice if we could try," she said. She pulled back her sleeve, revealing a rather battered wristwatch. "I'd better go and sort out the table linen."

Alice made her way back to the kitchen. She really would have to find a way to make it up to Félicité. In the meantime, she had to prepare the *petit fours* that would be served with coffee after dinner. She swept a handful of icing sugar across her worktop. As she rolled out the buttery yellow marzipan, she ticked off everything she had learned in the short time she was in the dining carriage, dabbing dots into the sugar-dusted worktop to help her remember.

The most obvious suspects are the dancers, she thought. After all, they *had* been to all the places that Uncle Robert had said *L'Anguille* had visited. But then, if they were the spies would they be so open about their travels? And there were two of them. Could *L'Anguille* actually be two people? Then there was the older man with all the books. He had definitely been trying to hide something and he seemed very protective of his books. Alice thought of her own codebook and her hand instinctively went to pat the pocket where she was keeping it close by. Might there be something in those books that he wanted to keep secret? But maybe he had just thought she was nosy.

She was about to discount Penelope and her father, but she shouldn't really. Next time she was in the dining carriage she should try a little harder to get some information out of them. Or perhaps she could just quiz Penelope? She was much friendlier than her father.

Then there was the elegant woman, Stella Blyth. She was so confident and she was good at getting people to talk, both qualities that were useful to a spy. Was she really a journalist or was that just a cover? Alice must try to get her to talk about her work. She would be allowed into the dining room after dinner to help with the desserts and *petit fours*. She must keep an eye on Stella. For the moment, she was prime suspect.

Alice was just pouring food colours into small bowls ready to brush on to the row of miniature marzipan apples and pears in front of her when the train let out one of its tremendous whistles. They were pulling into Paris Lyon, where the train would pause to take on more passengers. Outside, Alice could hear the bustle of the station as the stewards loaded trolleys filled with suitcases into the luggage carriage and helped passengers to their seats.

A few moments later, the head of one of the stewards appeared at the serving hatch. "Fresh coffee, no milk, please," he said to Alice. "That strange journalist woman wants some taken to her cabin. No idea what she finds to write about, stuck in there, scribbling away at her notebooks with that funny handwriting of hers."

Alice's ears pricked up. "Funny how?" she asked, filling the coffee pot and placing it on a spare ring on the packed stove.

The steward rolled his eyes. "Indecipherable!" he said. "Women can't write. It's ridiculous, all this 'education for girls' nonsense. And now they've been given the vote! The woman's handwriting is nothing but scrawls and scribbles. There's no sense in it because there's no sense in here." He tapped the side of his head. Alice felt herself bristle but she kept smiling.

Vain people are useful, she thought. *It can be easy to persuade them to tell you things as they are always so keen to prove how much they know. Maman* would call it "buttering them up", the way you might butter up a cake tin to make it easier to get cake out of it. She heard the coffee pot begin to rattle and took down a cup and tray from a shelf.

"I suppose you were able to read them, though," she said. "It must have been easy for you."

The steward shrugged airily. "Scribbles. Weird dashes and dots. It looked a bit like the music that my little sister used to pore over. That's the sort of thing that interests girls, I suppose. That journalist woman likes it, anyway. I saw her slipping a couple of music books into her cupboard drawer when

I helped her on board. Not the sort of thing that interests a man, of course. Far too many important things in the world to think about. I didn't bother reading it."

So he couldn't read it, Alice thought. *But why? Was it a different language? No, he had mentioned dashes and dots. Could Stella be writing in code?*

"Anyway," said the steward, taking the tray from Alice and snapping his fingers for her to fetch the coffee pot. "Can't hang around here all day chatting. Some of us have *hard* work to do."

Her mother had been right. All it took sometimes was a little buttering up. Alice decided that her next task would be to get a look at Stella's notebook. In the meantime, there were dainty morsels to create. She picked up her paintbrush and dipped it into a bowl full of cornflower-blue liquid. Then she paused. If the train was going to be waiting at the station for a while, maybe there was something else she could do.

Alice took off her apron and folded it quickly into a bundle that she left on the edge of the counter. Then she slipped out of the kitchen and down towards the small cabin that she shared with Félicité.

She spun the combination on her case round till the latch clicked, then she rifled through the first layer of camisoles and cardigans till her hand closed on a small leather purse. Alice shook out a few coins then crept to the door of the carriage. Outside, the platform was busy with passengers and staff rushing to and fro. Alice climbed down the steps of the carriage and made a beeline for the station house.

The man behind the desk raised an eye but accepted the small pile of francs and pushed the phone towards her. Alice dialled the number and hoped that the man would lose interest in her before Uncle Robert answered.

"Hello, it's Mam'selle Éclair from the company of the Sapphire Express," she said crisply into the receiver. "Madame Fritte has asked me to inform you that she is very comfortable in her carriage and we will arrive in Monte Carlo as expected."

There was a low whistle from the other end of the line.

"So my Little Phantom is on board," Uncle Robert said.

"That is correct," replied Alice, careful to keep up the act of an organised member of staff, but wondering why Uncle Robert did not sound more surprised. This was answered almost immediately.

"I knew you would not be able to resist the challenge of getting on to that train."

Alice could almost hear him smiling down the phone line.

"Have you further instructions?" she asked.

"Only to take care," said Uncle Robert. "And make sure that the papers are in your possession before the spy gets off the train at Marseilles. That is of the utmost importance. Hold on to them carefully and I will meet you at Paris when you return tomorrow. Oh, and, Alice, do *not* open the package under any circumstances. The less you know of its contents the better if you are caught by our enemies."

"I will ensure that your instructions are carried out," Alice said. "Have you... Have you any special instructions? Guidance?"

She heard Uncle Robert chuckle. "Don't worry, Alice, you will do brilliantly. *L'Anguille* may appear to be confident or they may play the part of a nervous passenger with something to hide. Like I say, they are slippery. Be on your guard and suspect everyone. Remember all our spy games from when you were little? All the skills you have learned over the last few months? You will need to use them all, my Little Phantom, if you are to defeat *L'Anguille*. And remember, *trust no one*."

Alice felt her hand begin to tremble. *L'Anguille* could be anyone. And Marseilles? That gave her less than twelve hours to find the spy, on a train where she could be put off at the next stop any time for burning the caramel or being late with the *petit fours*. With a voice that projected all the confidence she did not feel, she said "You may rely upon us entirely." She heard the click as Uncle Robert ended the call.

"Goodness, that sounded important," said a voice behind her. Alice started and almost dropped the receiver back into its cradle, causing the man behind the desk to tut loudly and move it out of her reach.

It was Penelope, beaming from ear to ear. Alice eyed her carefully. How much had she heard? And why had she followed her? It seemed silly to suspect Penelope of being the spy, but then you never knew. "*Trust no one*," hissed Uncle Robert's voice at the back of her head.

"Why aren't you on the train?" asked Alice.

"I wanted a walk," Penelope said. "Papa has discovered there is a piano on board and is being ever so dreary about me practising like young ladies should, but there isn't a shred of decent music there. It's all stuffy old composers like Mozart, so I'm hiding on the platform. What are you up to?"

"Nothing," lied Alice. "I just needed to make a phone call."

"Oh, me too," Penelope said. "Wait for me, I won't be long."

Penelope didn't wait for an answer but strode over to the desk and presented her francs in return for the telephone. Alice turned away and studied a map of France on the back wall, tracing the route the train would take across the country, through the mountains down to Marseilles and the sea. Behind her she heard Penelope whispering into the receiver and the words made the hairs on her arms prickle.

"I think I've recognised someone..." Then Penelope's voice dropped too low for her to hear, however hard she strained her ears, and a few moments later Penelope had replaced the receiver and turned to smile at Alice. "All done," she said, tucking her arm through Alice's and leading her out on to the platform.

Alice's head was in a whirl. What had Penelope meant? Who had she recognised? And who was she talking to? Penelope seemed so earnest and friendly, but as the girl steered Alice across the busy platform, dodging through the crowd while talking nonstop about something to do with one of her school friends, Alice wondered, could this be an act?

They were nearing the train when one of the stewards pushing a trolley with a slightly wayward wheel hit a bump on the platform and the trolley jerked to the right. Penelope jumped sideways to avoid being hit by a falling suitcase and Alice, who had been rather lost in her thoughts, tripped over her foot, bumping into a woman standing by the carriage door and knocking her over.

"Oh, I'm most terribly sorry," Alice cried, jumping forwards to help. The woman turned her head and Alice saw that it was the journalist, Stella. Penelope and Alice helped her to her feet and she stood looking slightly stunned, patting down her pockets and looking around to see whether she had dropped anything.

"I'm quite all right. It's far too crowded on this platform," she began, and then froze as her hand reached her head. A coil of red hair had fallen across her shoulder. Her eyes widened and she started scanning the platform floor, frantically looking for something. Alice and Penelope looked round too, expecting to see a piece of sparkling jewellery that had been lost in the fall.

"My hairpin," she said. "Can either of you see my hairpin – oh!"

Alice followed her gaze and glimpsed something rolling away from them across the platform. Both she and Stella raced after it, ducking round stewards with luggage and passengers saying fond farewells. Alice lost sight of the pin as it rolled under the wheels of a large suitcase. She scanned the platform for it while Stella stepped round an embracing couple and caught sight of it just as it rolled under a bench at the end of the platform.

"There!" cried Stella, running towards the bench so fast that she almost hurtled into a man wheeling his suitcase across the platform. Stella did not even pause to apologise. Alice followed and by the time she caught up, Stella was hitching the hem of her skirt so that she could kneel down and reach under the bench.

"I'm sure I can get it," Alice cried, rather surprised that one of the Sapphire Express passengers would stoop to getting their clothes dirty by kneeling on the unswept platform and clawing about under a bench.

Alice knelt down. The pin had rolled all the way to the wall and was balancing precariously over the grid of a drain. As Alice had suspected, underneath the bench, the floor was absolutely filthy. She peered at the pin. It was wooden, shaped like a stiletto blade and not jewelled or engraved. If anything, it looked rather old and battered, so it was a mystery why anyone would make such a fuss about it.

"*When someone makes a big fuss over something small, then it's something big to them,*" her mother had once told her when she was sulking over the fussiness of a customer who insisted on a particular shade of blue for the flowers on a wedding cake. It had turned out to be the colour of her fiancé's eyes. The pin was clearly important to Stella.

Alice sighed. There was nothing else for it. She unbuttoned her crisp white jacket and laid it on the bench. Having seen how cross Henri was with Félicité when her uniform was ruined, there was no way that Alice was going to risk covering her sleeves with soot and dust. She lowered herself till she was lying with her face brushing the floor and she could almost reach the tip of the pin. She tried to shuffle further, but the bench was too low. Alice stretched her fingers as far as they could go and flicked at the pin. It flipped into the air, spun and, as it was about to disappear down the drain, Alice caught at it between her thumb and fingertip. She breathed a sigh of relief, choking as her breath stirred up a lungful of spider webs and dust.

"Got it!" she cried, shuffling back out on to the platform.

"Oh, my goodness," said Penelope. "What a state you are in!"

Alice looked down at her dress. It was covered in dust and cobwebs and what she thought might be discarded croissants from the station café. She hauled herself to her feet, slapping at her uniform to remove as much of the dirt as possible before she put her pristine jacket back over it. As she was peeling a cobweb off the cuff of her dress, she noticed that Stella was looking at her rather pointedly. Alice looked down at the wooden pin still clasped tightly in her palm. Close up, she saw that it was made up of six or seven flattened sides. Stella held out a hand for it and Alice placed it into her waiting palm.

"Thank you, Miss...?"

"Éclair," said Alice.

Stella seemed to pause, looking at Alice a little more keenly. Then, with a brief nod to Alice and Penelope, Stella turned away and strode down the platform towards the dining car, leaving Alice still brushing down her uniform and staring after her.

She had been right. There was nothing unusual or special about that wooden pin at all. It was just an ordinary hairpin.

So why was Stella so desperate to get it back?

CHAPTER
EIGHT

Alice sneaked on to the train using the door nearest the cabin she shared with Félicité. If she could give her uniform a quick wipe with a damp cloth, she might at least make it presentable. She had reached the top step when she saw the *maître d'* walking down the corridor, talking one of the stewards through the wine list for dinner. There was no way of hiding. Alice thought about ducking back down the steps, but it was too late, and the look on the *maître d'*s face showed that he had seen her.

"MAM'SELLE ÉCLAIR!"

The *maître d'* slammed shut the folder he was carrying and bore down on her, his face creased with anger. "What HAVE you done to your Sapphire Express uniform?"

"I... I was helping a passenger with something they had lost," Alice said.

"You should not have been off the train at all," the *maître d'* snapped. "Staff are forbidden to leave the train except at the express permission of me, the driver or Chef Henri."

"I saw her in some distress from the train," Alice lied. "I thought it best to help. She had lost something precious under one of the platform benches."

The *maître d'* waved away her explanation.

"You understand, Mam'selle Éclair, that your position on this train is precarious. This is not the behaviour we expect from the staff of the Sapphire Express." He drew a fob watch out of a pocket in his waistcoat and clicked it open. "The train departs in twenty minutes, Mam'selle Éclair," he said. "We should arrive in Laroche shortly after dinner, where there will be plenty of trains back to Paris, should it be decided that you are no longer a good fit with the Sapphire Express."

Alice hurried back to the kitchen, hoping that her face was not as flushed as it felt. Somehow her cheeks were on fire but there was a cold pebble somewhere in her stomach. She *had* to impress the *maître d'* with her *petits fours* or Laroche would be the end of her mission.

Alice had always prided herself that her *petits fours* were the finest in Paris, but that might not be enough. These had to be the best in *France*. It was all down to attention to detail, and Michelangelo painting the Sistine Chapel could not have been in as rapt concentration as Alice was for the next hour, applying tiny brushstrokes of food colouring to the marzipan shapes in front of her.

Around her, the kitchen was a-bustle, with Jacques and the other chefs combining flavours with the precision of perfumers creating the perfect scent. Henri moved silently from one workstation to another, tweaking and scolding, fixing and praising. When he passed Alice's station he did not offer advice or ask to taste anything, but Alice heard him pause and whisper "*Très bien*" to himself before moving on. She breathed a little easier. Perhaps she *wouldn't* be thrown off the train at the next stop after all.

Alice was crumbling chocolate into a bowl, ready to be melted, when she heard her name being hissed. She looked up and saw Penelope's face peering over the counter where Jacques would shortly begin to plate up the starters. Alice slipped over to her, glad that everyone was engrossed in their work and hoping that Henri did not look up from showing the *sauté chef* the perfect consistency for the onion sauce.

"Penelope!" Alice whispered. "You shouldn't be here. How did you get past the steward?"

Penelope waved a hand casually. "Oh, him! He's busy helping Papa search for one of his cufflinks. Papa's always losing them, so it's ever so easy to create a distraction by hiding one. I wanted to see what you were up to. Goodness, it's crowded in there!"

Penelope leaned over the counter and stuck her head fully into the narrow kitchen.

Alice looked round in alarm. "Please," she said. "It's lovely to see you, but we can't have visitors. I'm already in trouble for being off the train earlier. I can't afford to break any more rules or I might get the sack."

Penelope instantly pulled herself back into the corridor and ducked out of sight so quickly that Alice had to clamp her hand over her mouth to stop herself from laughing.

"We can't have that at all," came Penelope's whispered voice from below the counter. "Only I was so *bored*, and I wanted to give you the most delicious gossip about Jake and Irving. I told my friend Pip I'd seen them again when I phoned her from the station. She's mad with envy and furious that she's not here herself."

Alice paused. So Penelope had simply been calling a friend. And she was keen to share information with Alice about the other passengers. Alice swept away her suspicions about Penelope. The girl simply wanted to share some gossip, and gossip was always useful to a spy. Alice glanced round once more. Everyone else was absorbed in their work so she slipped into the corridor and hastened Penelope along to the door by the dining car. Once the two girls were bundled into a corner, Penelope started to spill.

"I've been thinking that they seemed awfully familiar," she gushed. "And then I realised why! Papa and I were at Le Touquet this year. Papa wouldn't let me go *anywhere* fun and by the second week I was simply *bursting* to go to one of the parties that everyone talked about at breakfast, so I waited till Papa was asleep and then I sneaked out with Pip Montague – she's my best school friend, you know. She and her people were staying in the same hotel as us and she pretended to have a headache, so they left her in her room and we went to a dancehall in the middle of the town and didn't get back till three in the morning!"

"And Jake and Irving were dancing?" said Alice. She had all sorts of questions about the dance and the dresses and she was just a little envious that Penelope had managed to do something so exciting, but she needed to focus. Someone else had mentioned Le Touquet today. Who was it?

"No!" said Penelope. "We didn't see them at the dance. We saw them in the hotel. We were slipping past the concierge to get back to our rooms, and on the way through the lobby we saw Jake and Irving. I *know* it was them because Pip had seen them at breakfast and had said how handsome they both were. Well, the odd thing was that as we were creeping in, *they* were creeping out."

"At three in the morning?" Alice asked. This *did* seem like peculiar behaviour.

"That's not all," squeaked Penelope, clearly getting to the most exciting part. "The next day, Lady Homburg discovered that her priceless tiara had gone missing. And a roll of notes from the room of some stuffy old Viscount, and a pair of ridiculously valuable ruby hairclips belonging to Lady Connie Whittaker. Oh, and a simply HUGE emerald brooch, the size of a partridge egg! And Jake and Irving *never came back to the hotel."*

Penelope stood back and looked at Alice with an expression that said, "What do you think of that, then?"

"So you think they are jewel thieves?" asked Alice.

"Well, it's a possibility," said Penelope. "And I thought, wouldn't it be amazing if I could help unmask them? I've always wanted to be a detective. I've read simply heaps of books. Would you help? Pip Montague said it might be too dangerous to try to do it all myself."

Alice's mind was racing. Penelope's phone call had been a bit of gossip to her best friend, and she was probably entirely wrong about Jake and Irving and the jewels. But really Penelope had been rather clever, working out how to distract her father *and* the eagle eyes of the Sapphire Express train staff. *It would be lovely to take her into my confidence and work as a team,* thought Alice. Her uncle's voice resounded in her ears in response: "*Trust no one*". But Penelope seemed so *innocent*, and if she thought she was tracking down a jewel thief, Alice might be able to get more information on the passengers out of her.

Oh dear, thought Alice. *That feels a bit like I'm using her.*

"Mam'selle Éclair!" Alice jumped at the sound of Henri calling for her. She gave Penelope a gentle push towards the dining carriage.

"You'd better go. Keep an eye on Jake and Irving and tell me anything you think might be odd. *Anything*, you understand? We can compare notes later."

As Penelope dashed back to her cabin, Alice remembered who else had recognised Jake and Irving at Le Touquet. Stella had seen them too, and they had lied and said they had never been there.

So were they really jewel thieves, or something even worse?

CHAPTER
NINE

The rest of the time before dinner passed in a flurry of activity. The chefs whisked, stirred and sprinkled till the air was thick with the combination of scents – sharp, tangy garlic and sweet lemon cream, warm onion and spicy cardamom. The train itself seemed aware of the urgency as it pelted along at top speed, building up a good head of steam before the hills of Burgundy.

By the time the fish course was being served, Alice had changed her mind about who her main suspect was a dozen times. She had given little thought to Mr Fulmington, but the older man, whom she had heard the *maîtré d'* refer to as "the professor", seemed very secretive about what was in his books (though not secretive enough to lock them safely in his compartment). Surely if he really were the spy, he would have them under lock and key?

Jake and Irving were a better bet. There was certainly something very strange going on with their behaviour about Le Touquet. But then the steward had mentioned that odd writing of Stella's. Perhaps she was writing in code? Alice wracked her brains trying to think of a way to get a glimpse at the woman's notebooks, which then made her feel quite faint at the thought of anyone getting sight of her *own* notebooks. She was so distracted that she nearly dropped the tray of crystal glasses containing perfectly set *crème au chocolat* that Chef Albert had whisked to perfection. It was his signature dish and, to his annoyance, Alice had been given the task of creating a chocolate medallion to accompany each dessert. She had forty minutes while the main course was served to create something beautiful enough to impress even him.

She planned to use her piping tools to create the route of the Sapphire Express across the six crystal glasses of creamy dessert that were set before her on the counter. She bent her head low over her workstation and began fashioning white chocolate into dainty, thin discs, then she piped on them the curves of the mountains they were passing through. A whisk of her piping bag and a river appeared, crossing from one medallion to the next. A few quick dots and the city of Laroche was created on the *chocolat* intended for Penelope. Stella's *chocolat* was the grandest of them all. Alice worked methodically, building up layer upon layer of chocolate until the Sapphire Express itself stood in the middle of the medallion, the merest hint of smoke blowing from its perfectly piped funnel in a smear of whisper-thin chocolate. She had almost finished it, when she thought about Stella's notebook with the "scribbles". *What if it was really a code?*

Alice paused. What she was considering was a risk, but she had so little time, she needed to make a move. She picked up her piping bag and iced "Sapphire Express" in Morse code around the edge of the medallion. She would need to watch Stella's reaction carefully. A spy would recognise Morse at once.

Alice stood up, her back aching a little from being bent over for so long. She glanced at the clock high on the galley wall, picked up the medallions and, one by one, balanced them on top of the *crème au chocolat*. Then she turned to Henri.

"Ready, Chef," she declared.

The dining carriage seemed different in the light of evening. The lacquered wooden walls gleamed in the lamplight, their delicate inlays catching the flickering light of the candles on each table.

Everything was polished to perfection, from the brass fittings to the crystal decanters and intricately cut champagne flutes. The stewards, brisk and attentive in their crisp white and blue tunics, moved like perfectly mannered ghosts from table to table, topping up glasses and whisking away plates with such skill that they were hardly noticed.

The passengers were in high spirits. Penelope sat demurely in a pretty evening dress of fluted chiffon, and Alice had no doubt that the tiny flickers of light at her ears were real diamonds. The men, of course, were rather boringly attired in dinner jackets, except for Jake, who wore a cream lounge suit with navy-blue trim and a waistcoat of particularly striking eal-shot silk. Alice made her way through the carriage, carefully placing the dainty glasses of dessert in front of the passengers. When she got to the table where Stella had been, her seat was empty.

"Madame has gone to her cabin," the steward told her. "Serve the passengers here and then take hers through to her. She is in compartment three."

Alice nodded. To get to the corridor where the passengers' sleeping compartments were, she had to pass through the Sapphire Express's bar. It was as glamorous as the dining carriage. Plush sofas plumped full of cushions sat around the edge. There were walnut lacquered tables decorated with vases of fresh roses, and at the end of the carriage was the long bar, behind which the bartender, Monsieur Ames, was polishing already sparkling glassware and setting up for when the guests would retire after dinner. Alice nodded politely to him and passed through the door to the sleeping compartments.

Outside compartment number three, Alice took a deep breath. She would only have a few moments inside and she would need to be prepared to take in as many clues as possible. She knocked and, on hearing Stella's voice, opened the door.

For a second Alice was so overcome by how luxurious the room was that she forgot to look for anything. The sleeping compartments in First Class were panelled in the same exquisite wood and lacquer as the dining car and bar. A generously padded banquette, upholstered in sumptuous blue silk velvet, ran the length of the compartment, with a nightstand on which stood an elaborate glass lantern, a vase full of fresh roses, and a silver tray for bonbons and tiny cups of hot chocolate.

Stella lounged across the seat, effortlessly poured into a blood-red halterneck gown. She wore no jewels except for a single ring with an egg-shaped ruby set in a channel of jet. Alice set the dessert dish in front of Stella and glanced quickly round. Stella, she decided, was messy. An open suitcase spilled silk blouses and scarves across the small table by the window. The door to her bathroom was ajar and, beyond it, Alice could see a satin robe discarded on the floor. It all reminded her of something, but she couldn't quite put her finger on it.

Stella gave a low chuckle and picked up the tiny chocolate engine between her long scarlet nails. Alice watched her face, waiting for a flash of recognition as she saw the Morse code, but Stella merely raised an eyebrow before taking a small nibble out of the side. "Delicious," she said.

Alice smiled politely, but this was quite frustrating. *I'm no nearer to knowing whether she's the spy or not,* she thought. *And I've got no good reason to stay and ask questions.*

She turned to go, then froze as her eye fell on the clear-glass coffee table by the cabin's couch.

Laid facedown and open was a notebook and a slim pencil. If only she could catch a glimpse of what was in it, but she could hardly hope to distract the woman enough to pick it up.

Think, Alice said to herself, as the train rounded a corner, its whistle sounding shrilly. Alice glanced out at the night as it flew past, the lights of small towns twinkling in the darkness and reflecting off the window. *Of course.*

As the train righted itself, Alice pretended to lose her balance and dropped her tray at just the right angle for it to fall beneath the glass table. Both she and Stella moved quickly to pick it up and Alice had the merest glimpse of the writing on the notebook, reflected in the shining silver. The steward had been right, it was just scrawls, but Alice knew what those scrawls meant. Years before, Uncle Robert had taught her shorthand. It could be very useful for taking field notes, especially if one was on public transport with nosy neighbours. The first mark on the paper was a thin curved stroke that Alice knew was an "E". Then came the loop of an "F", an "N" and another that could be an "F" or an "I". She quickly memorised the rest before Stella snatched the tray up and handed it back to her.

E.F.N.I.I.U.D.E.G.G.F.S…

Alice nodded her thanks and backed out of the cabin, her heart beating fast against her ribs. She was sure that she had read the letters correctly. She was excellent at shorthand. But they made no sense, unless – of course – Stella was writing in code, and that meant that Stella might well be the spy.

And there was something else that was suspicious. Stella had been very eager to pick up the tray. A customer would never stoop to help a member of staff without good reason, and Alice was sure she knew what Stella's reason was – she had not wanted anyone to see inside her notebook.

As she made her way back to the kitchen, Alice ran over the letters in her head. She must not forget them. On her way through the dining carriage, she caught Penelope's eye and the girl frowned rather dramatically and shook her head. Clearly her investigations of Jake and Irving had gone no further, but Alice was too caught up in her own investigation to care. She wanted to sneak off to her own cabin and write down Stella's message, but as she entered the passageway by the kitchen, Henri called her in with a list of jobs that she could help with, beginning with preparing the dough for fresh croissants the next morning. Alice sighed and went to her workstation.

She swept a generous handful of flour across her counter and reached for a water jug. She was just looking for the yeast pot when a thought occurred to her. She picked up a wooden skewer from the counter and, keeping her writing as small as possible, wrote out the letters in the flour on the worktop and stared at them while she began to mix her dough.

CHAPTER
TEN

Twenty minutes later, Alice slammed the croissant dough against the counter in frustration, throwing up clouds of flour that smeared the letters she had drawn and made Henri turn from his job of calculating which provisions they would need to reorder for the return journey. Alice huffed upwards to blow the flour out of her eyes. Whatever cipher Stella was using, it was unbreakable. She could spot no patterns that might give her a clue how to crack it and the cipher remained stubbornly locked to her, little more than a jumble of unrelated letters.

There's nothing for it, she thought. *I'll just HAVE to get into her cabin and do a proper search.*

Alice worked quickly, folding the dough into perfect croissants that she left to rise under a cloth on the warm stove. Then she swept the countertop, making sure that she obliterated any sign of the writing, before slipping into the corridor. She could hear the pianist in the First Class bar and the unmistakable bell sounds of champagne bottles on crystal flutes. Monsieur Ames would be mixing his famous cocktails. She could check who was in the bar and then search their compartments. But to do that meant getting into the bar again, and she had no excuse for being there.

She took a pile of glass cloths from the counter by the kitchen door. They were neatly laundered and the perfect cover. Alice folded them over her arm and strode down the train towards the dining car. Two of the stewards were clearing the tables, changing wine glasses and dessert plates for bone china breakfast cups. Alice drifted past them, her eyes on the door to the bar at the end of the carriage.

"Yes, Mam'selle, can I help?" The steward by the door was polite but icily cold.

"I brought some fresh glass cloths for Monsieur Ames," Alice said, waving towards the white linen squares draped over her arm. The steward frowned.

"I can give him those," he said, whisking the cloths away from Alice before she could stop him.

Alice opened her mouth to object, but it was no use. Before the door to the bar closed on her she caught a glimpse of the party inside. Most of the customers stood by the bar, where Monsieur Ames was shaking a silver cocktail shaker, the ice cubes rattling noisily in time with the clatter of the train against the rails. Stella was leaning over the piano in the middle of the carriage leafing through a pile of sheet music. The professor was perched rather uncomfortably on a stool, hugging his red book to his chest and talking with Penelope, who was sipping a glass of something sweet-looking. As soon as Penelope spotted Alice, she jumped off her seat and dashed over.

"Big news!" she said, bustling into the corridor. "I mentioned to Papa that I wanted to go back to Le Touquet this summer and Jake spilled his drink all over himself. He claimed that the train juddered but we were going quite slowly uphill and it was as steady as Pip Montague's hand with a lacrosse stick. I'm *sure* they are jewel thieves. Do you think we should search their compartment?"

Alice thought for a moment. Penelope was far too loud and excitable to poke around in the compartments without being discovered, and then Alice's game would be up too. But this was her chance to make a proper search of Stella's things, and it would be easier if she didn't have to be on the lookout for any Sapphire Express staff or Stella herself.

"If they found you there, they'd smell a rat," she said. "I'm staff. I'll do it. But if you keep watch in the bar, you could warn me if they come through. I'm not *really* meant to be in the compartments, but I'm sure I could come up with an excuse if I absolutely have to."

Penelope nodded. "When?"

Alice frowned. It was clear that she was not going to get past the steward at the door very easily. It would be different if she was carrying food. Alice's brow furrowed as the beginning of an idea appeared in her mind. "Give me half an hour," she said. "When I arrive, you can help me distract the steward, but for now you'd better go back in before I get into trouble for talking to passengers."

Penelope rolled her eyes. "Urgh, must I? The music in here is so *old*! All those composers that we are meant to learn about at school. Stella insists on choosing it. The pianist has been playing for her all evening. She even brought her own music! The cheek of it!"

Alice smiled at Penelope's evident outrage. She waved her back into the bar and, pulling the door closed, made her way back to the kitchen. The only task remaining for the evening was to finish the croissants and *pain au chocolat* so that they could be baked fresh in the morning for breakfast. Neither of those would be needed in the bar so late, though, and it was no use coming up with a new drink that the passengers simply *must* try. The Sapphire Express's barman, Ames, was the expert there. Besides which, Alice did not know the slightest thing about cocktails. People didn't eat when they were having cocktails, did they?

Of course, just because people didn't *usually* do something didn't mean they couldn't be *persuaded* to…

Alice quickened her steps and began to run the contents of the galley store cupboards through her mind, pairing pots of almond paste and rosewater essence. By the time she reached the kitchen, Alice was itching to get started on her plan.

An hour later, Alice was looking down at two plates of exquisite tiny biscuits arranged on a paper doily on the galley counter. There were delicately scented lavender biscuits, tiny star-shaped bites of punchy clementine and sumptuous dark chocolate roundels that would cut across the sharper cocktails. There were savoury wafers flavoured with rosemary and rich cheeses with a sprinkling of sea salt. Alice knew that each and every one of them would melt like butter in the mouth. Now she had to hope that she could get them past the steward who guarded the bar door.

She picked up the trays and was halfway down the corridor to the bar when she had an idea. She left the trays on a table in the dining car, dashed to the cabin she shared with Félicité and looked round the door. Félicité was lying on her bunk, reading a fashion magazine.

"Psst, are you busy?" whispered Alice.

"Not especially," said Félicité. "I have to help fold the linen for breakfast in half an hour, but Chef has allowed me a break so I thought I'd have a quick read. Just look at this music gala at the Musée d'Orsay last month. The dresses are *incredible!*"

She held the magazine up to Alice, who smiled broadly.

"Would you like to see some real dresses?" she asked.

Alice strode down the corridor towards the steward guarding the bar, her chin lifted high with the air of someone who had *definitely* informed the *maître d'* or Chef Henri of what she was doing and had most definitely *not* simply gone ahead without permission.

"We're to pass these round the guests," she said firmly.

The steward eyed her warily, but he pushed the door open so Alice could enter. Félicité followed close behind her and Alice smiled as she heard the girl gasp with delight at the sight of Stella and Penelope in their finest frocks.

"Cocktail biscuits," Alice declared to Monsieur Ames, who was shaking fruit juices together to create one of his signature drinks. "Quite the thing in Paris at the moment." With one final flourish the barman set the silver and crystal cocktail shaker on the bar and filled a sugar-rimmed glass with a frothing pink liquid.

"For Mam'selle," Ames said, smiling at Penelope "I hope this one will be even more to your liking."

Penelope took the concoction and sipped it

eagerly before smiling happily at Ames. Alice had been right. Like all members of the Sapphire Express staff, he was a master of his craft.

"Oh, it's delicious," she beamed. "Sweet but not *too* sweet."

She grinned at Alice and under her breath whispered, "You got in!"

Alice nodded. She selected one of the lavender and rosewater squares that she knew would complement the cocktail that Ames had created.

"Try it with this, Mam'selle," she said, a little louder than necessary, passing the sweet treat to Penelope on a teaspoon. Penelope took a tiny bite and then quickly finished the rest.

"Oh, these are delicious!" she cried, waving everyone towards where Alice and Félicité were standing with the trays. "Everyone, you must try these!"

Penelope really was rather wonderful, thought Alice, as the passengers gathered round her and she gushed about the amazing treats that Alice and Félicité had brought through. It was enough of a diversion for Alice to leave her tray on the bar and slip away through the door to the cabins. She took a glance back and, to her delight, saw Félicité gawping in open admiration at Stella's dress, and the smile on her face could not have been wider.

CHAPTER
ELEVEN

Alice pushed open the door to compartment number three and stepped inside. In the background she could hear the pianist in the bar striking up another genteel piece and Stella demanding something with "a bit more zip".

"Play that piece you I gave you earlier!" she cried. "It's from my favourite opera in the world. I saw it in Milan last year and I know you have the music. It was on the piano." A moment later a brisk tune cascaded through the train and Alice heard the sound of Jake and Irving kicking up their heels and peals of laughter from the others. She did not think that Penelope would need to warn her that anyone was coming too soon.

Stella's compartment was tidier than it had been before. Her exquisitely tailored blouses and suits were carefully arranged on the rail by the couch, and a pile of notebooks stood in a neat pile from largest to smallest on the nightstand, but the muddle of scarves tied round the handle of the top drawer showed that she had not entirely tidied up. A memory twitched at the back of Alice's brain. Where *had* she seen that before?

Alice flicked through the notebooks, but none

of them was written in the peculiar shorthand code that Stella had been using. There were lists of clothing, evidently an aid to packing, an account of a soirée at the French ambassador's house and a letter from Stella's mother that Alice closed the book on. There was no need to poke her nose into people's personal affairs unnecessarily.

She turned her attention to the drawers of the nightstand, expecting them to be locked, but they were open. Moving a book of pieces by Mozart, Alice discovered Stella's passport and – oh! – the places the woman had been. Austria, England and Germany were all there, but also Italy, Spain, Turkey, America and so many more. Her passport was peppered with stamps from all over the world and crammed full of papers welcoming her and granting her safe passage. Alice felt a flush of envy course through her, soon replaced by a realisation that such a passport could easily belong to *L'Anguille*. All the places in Stella's passport were places that the treacherous spy had been. But then, Stella was a journalist too. Wouldn't that be why she was so well travelled? Or was that merely a cover?

Alice replaced the passport and pushed her hand

deeper into the drawer. Her fingers brushed against something soft and velvety and she pulled out a parcel of pink velvet tied up in a black silk cord. She sat on the couch with the parcel on her lap and carefully untied the cord. The velvet unrolled with ease, revealing a smart black lacquerware jewel case. Alice examined the front, hoping for an easily pickable lock, but the case had seven dials on the front, each displaying a letter. "ADOSGPE," she read, frowning. The dials had clearly been spun into random formation after the case was locked, and a brief tug at the top of the case confirmed this.

So what could the word be?

"*Nothing is ever random*," said Uncle Robert in her ear. It had been his favourite mantra in all the notes he had left her. Anything could be deduced by observing. People never liked to stray too far from what they loved when hiding secrets. Agents used the names of favourite nieces or pets, book characters and songs. *If I only knew Stella better, I might have a chance of working out what word she is using*, thought Alice. Without much real hope, she spun the dials round to "JOURNAL" and tried the lock.

"Well, that was *never* going to work," she told herself scornfully. She sat back against the pillows and glared at the box. What *did* she know about Stella? Closing her eyes for a moment, she pictured her in the bar, dressed in her long shimmering gown, a sparkling drink in her hand, laughing, leafing through the pianist's sheet music and demanding her favourite pieces. She was a bold, fearless bolt of life. She was a writer. She was a traveller. She was someone Alice *longed* to be, but who was she really, deep down? What might she hide her secrets in? Why was Alice thinking of music? She snapped upright, straining her ears for the silence that would mean that the party in the bar was closing down, but to her relief she could hear, faintly, the notes of the piano. The poor pianist must be feeling so tired by now. Stella was keeping him very busy indeed.

Alice glanced at the book of Mozart arias in the drawer. She remembered the steward mentioning that she had brought music on board, but why? Did she play or sing? Alice felt a flutter of excitement rise in her chest. The music. Could that be the answer? It was a long shot, but she had to try. *"Mozart" is six letters*, she thought. *"Music" is five. "Orchestra" is nine...*

Alice frowned, but the spark of excitement refused to go away and if Alice Éclair knew one thing it was that she could trust her gut. There *was* something about music, if only she could work it out.

She stood up and smoothed down the coverlet on the banquette. If she was going to work out Stella's secret, then she was going to have to go back to the bar.

CHAPTER
TWELVE

Alice crept back along the corridor and slipped inside the door to the bar. The pianist was playing something soft and lilting, his hands dancing across the keys. He looked utterly bored. Ames was whisking a cloth across the cut-glass bar. The passengers were gathered round a table where Stella was talking to Jake and Irving about how much they must love performing. Feeling a little guilty that she had not even begun to look in their cabin, Alice shot a look at Penelope that said, "Cover for me," and Penelope started to gush about how much she loved Stella's jewellery. Félicité, holding two empty trays, dashed across to her. "I've had such a *wonderful* time," she whispered. "Thank you so much! I'm going to take these back to the kitchen and then I'm going to write ALL of it down in my journal. I might be able to draw Miss Fulmington's frock too. I think I have just the right shade of pink pencil in my case. Did I tell you I like to draw?"

Alice beamed as Félicité gushed. She was glad she had made it up to her for spoiling things earlier. She took the trays from her and ushered her towards the door. "I'll take these to the kitchen," she said. "You go back to the cabin."

Félicité squeezed her hand and dashed out of the door, no doubt already running through the evening all over again in her mind.

Alice made her way across to the piano and began to casually collect up the sheet music that lay strewn across its top. There were fast pieces where the notes were falling over one another to fit on the stave, and slower ones where the music looked half bare and the notation was simple and designed to be played with great emotion. Alice flicked through them, looking for something, anything, that might link them together. Perhaps they all began with the same set of notes? Might that be it?

"Thanks for that," whispered the pianist. "I've done nothing but play Rossini all evening, because of that woman over there. She brought her own music, would you believe it? The show people wanted a bit of jazz, but other than that..." He raised an eyebrow at the pile of music in Alice's hands.

Alice's mind was racing. Rossini. Seven letters. Could she hope?

Behind her she heard Stella put her glass down on the table.

"Well, that's me done for the night," she

announced. "I think I'll turn in."

Alice froze and dashed a desperate look at Penelope.

"Oh, but you can't," Penelope cried. "You promised me you would teach me how to win at Patience. I can never make the cards come right."

Penelope pulled her best "disappointed" look and Stella let out a sigh. "Oh, all right then, twenty minutes, but I really must turn in soon. We'll be in Nice in the morning and I need to be fresh as a daisy."

They sat at a table and Ames produced a deck of cards seemingly from nowhere with the smoothness for which the Sapphire Express stewards were famous. Stella shuffled the cards from one hand to another, lifting her palm high above the table and letting them cascade from one hand to the other. Her fingers moved nimbly, chopping the deck in half, splitting and fanning the cards so that they were a blur. Penelope marvelled at her.

Alice mouthed "brilliant" at Penelope, crept back through the door and dashed towards Stella's compartment.

You don't have much time, she told herself, pulling

open the drawer and taking out the jewel box. She spun the dials round.

"ROSS"

Please work.

"ROSSIN"

Please.

"ROSSINI"

Alice held her breath and pushed her finger against the lock.

And, with a click so clear that she was certain it must be heard throughout the entire train, it sprang open.

Alice pulled back the lid. Inside lay a parcel wrapped in brown paper and sturdy twine. The papers. It must be! Alice tugged at the knot but the twine held firm.

There was nothing for it, she must take the parcel. Alice reached in and her fingers brushed against something else in the box, tucked away in a fold of the velvet lining. It was the wooden hairpin that Stella had been so keen to retrieve from under the bench. Alice squeezed her eyes shut and pictured Stella in the bar. Her red hair had been held in place with a ruby and jet barrette. Stella owned some gorgeous jewels, so why would she lock this plain, wooden hairpin securely in her case? Alice pocketed it and tried to fit the parcel of papers in after it. But the package was too big and her fingers fumbled. The parcel flew from her grasp, bounced against the nightstand, caught on the edge of the drawer, and Alice heard the paper tear. The tightly knotted binding sprang back and papers spilled out all over the floor.

"*No*!" Alice hissed, dropping to her knees and scrabbling to gather the papers. She had been right. They *were* passports. Passports and security papers, dozens of them. Stella was the spy, passing documents to agents so they could enter France. Alice felt hot fury spike through herself. How dare this woman gaily drink champagne and play cards while all the time she was plotting to betray France and help her enemies? Alice swiped at a folded security paper and ripped it open, eager to see the face of the traitor she was about to bring down.

From the paper in her hand stared the face of a small girl.

CHAPTER
THIRTEEN

Alice froze. There must be some mistake. She reached out for one of the passports and opened it. It was for an elderly woman of eighty-two. Alice dropped it and reached for another, a set of papers belonging to a woman in her thirties and her three children. None of this made sense. She became more frantic, tearing open papers and passports that revealed children, elderly couples, whole families, babies. She felt her head swim with confusion. Surely these people could not be spies?

Down the corridor, Alice heard the music in the bar stop. How long had she sat there? She must hurry. She scrabbled the papers together, stuffing them into the front of her jacket and buttoning it up. Then she closed the drawer, smoothed down the coverlet on the banquette and slipped out of the door, just in time to bump into Penelope.

"You've been an age!" Penelope exclaimed. "We played three rounds of Patience and I stalled them for as long as I could but now the party's breaking up. Quick, hide in here while I get rid of Papa." And she hurried Alice along the carriage to compartment number six, pushed her inside and shut the door on her.

Alice glanced around. A rather tatty bunny was sat on the banquette, next to a straw boater and a pile of books. It was clearly Penelope's compartment. Outside, she heard Penelope saying goodnight to her father and promising to be up early for breakfast.

Alice sat down and stared at the ceiling, trying to make sense of everything.

There must be something in the papers I'm missing, she thought. *Uncle Robert said there were dozens of spies who would use these papers, but most of the people in them are old or children.*

She had heard tales of children being made to join government programmes where they would be brainwashed into thinking they were doing the right thing for their country, but some of the children in the papers were so young. She could not imagine that the enemy was using them as spies. What about the babies?

Alice drew one of the identity papers out of her jacket. It was for a Mrs Berkley. She was seventy-six and looked very frail. She had the kind eyes that Alice's grandmother had. Alice gazed into them and felt more troubled than ever. Surely this woman could not be a spy. But if these weren't the papers that her uncle needed to find, then what were they? It would be absurd to think that there was someone else on the train with a parcel of identity papers and passports…

You've missed things before, Alice, she told herself. *You're missing something now. Maybe these aren't the papers you're looking for?*

She was still staring at the paper when the door was thrown open and Penelope careered into the room. Alice stuffed the paper out of sight and moved up to make space on the banquette for her.

"What did you find?" Penelope demanded.

Alice's heart sank. She hadn't even *looked* in Jake and Irving's room and now Penelope would demand to know what she had been doing. She could lie and say she found nothing, but, looking into Penelope's eager, trusting face, Alice found that the lie died on her lips.

"I'm sorry, Penelope," she sighed. "I got distracted and I didn't manage to search."

Penelope's face fell. "What on earth have you been *doing*, then? I've been pretending to learn Patience and having to be hopeless at it, when actually I'm very good indeed and it was *me* who managed to teach Pip Montague when everyone else at school had given up on her. You can't imagine how tedious it is, pretending to be something you're not."

Alice bit her lip to stop herself from laughing at that. "I really am sorry," she said.

"I'm sure it's them," Penelope said. "I definitely saw them at Le Touquet and they never like to talk about it. I've worked it into conversation a dozen times. Papa thinks I'm obsessed. He's promised to book a fortnight there next summer the minute we get off the train."

"And Stella saw them too," said Alice. "She mentioned it to them the first time they met and they denied they were ever there."

"Well, there you are," said Penelope. "What more proof do we need? And there's another thing. There have been other jewel thefts this year at the big resorts. The professor – you know, the nice elderly gentleman with all the books? – he mentioned it. That was quite a surprise really, because he didn't look the type to be interested in jewels, but the minute I mentioned Le Touquet, he started to talk about the robberies. And what do you know, the very next place that Jake and Irving mentioned performing at, the professor said that there had been thefts there too!"

Alice frowned. It really did look as though Jake and Irving were jewel thieves. Penelope was right. Could they be spies too? It was possible, of course. People who were dishonest in one way were often dishonest in others. And if the papers that she was looking for weren't the ones in Stella's compartment, then where were they?

"Well, they are safely tucked up in bed, so we won't be able to search their compartment till tomorrow," sulked Penelope. "What a swizz. I'm sure it's them."

Alice looked over at Penelope's pink velvet jewel case sitting on her nightstand.

"Nonsense," she said. "We're going to search that compartment tonight."

It took ten minutes to work out a plan. Alice secured the papers from Stella's compartment safely inside her uniform and together she and Penelope slipped into the corridor and moved down to outside Jake and Irving's compartment.

"Excuse me," said Penelope, leaning in close to the door so that her voice could be heard inside.

"Would you be able to help me?"

"Of course, Mam'selle," said Alice in her best "Sapphire Express" voice. "It is very late, though. Should you not be asleep? I can fetch extra pillows if that is what you need."

Penelope looked as though she was about to burst into giggles and Alice had to glare at her very sternly. They needed to concentrate if this was to work. Penelope mouthed "sorry" at her and went back to their agreed script.

"Not at all. It's just that I've lost the diamond barrette that I was wearing in my hair earlier. It's quite a tiny thing but worth rather a lot of money. The diamonds are from a royal crown, you see, set in platinum. Papa will be in a terrible temper if he knows it's missing. I think I might have lost it in the bar. Would you be able to help?"

"Of course, Mam'selle," said Alice. She crossed her fingers tightly behind her back. Would they take the bait? "I will follow you shortly. I just need to check up on one thing in the kitchen."

"I will meet you there in ten minutes, then," said Penelope. "I'm quite sure it's in there, but I should double-check my room first, I suppose. I'm such a ninny!"

Alice gave a nod and the two girls scuttled back to Penelope's compartment. Then they waited with the door open a crack, watching to see if Jake and Irving took the bait.

After a few moments, they heard the click of one of the compartment doors further down the train, away from Jake and Irving's room. Alice stared as the professor stepped out and, with soft, shuffling footsteps, made his way towards the bar.

"The professor!" hissed Penelope. "Surely it can't be him!"

Alice's head whirled. Of all the people to be a jewel thief, she had not expected the professor. She motioned to Penelope to follow her and, together, they crept out into the corridor and hastened down to compartment four.

"He probably locked it behind him," said Penelope, but before she could begin to ask how they would solve that, Alice had taken out her lockpick tools and begun working at the lock. She saw Penelope's eyes widen as the compartment door clicked open.

"Best if you don't ask," she said, stepping inside.

She glanced round. The professor's room was much tidier than Stella's. A heavy dictionary and pile of notebooks sat neatly stacked on the table. The professor's luggage, a large carpet bag, stood by the window.

Alice went straight to the nightstand and tried the drawer. It was locked. Hoping that they had sufficient time while the professor was in the bar, looking for Penelope's barrette, she went to work on it with her tools. She could feel Penelope's eyes boring into her, wanting desperately to ask where she learned such a trick. After a few minutes she felt the lock give and the drawer sprang open, but there was nothing in there except a red leather book. Alice recognised it at once. It was the one that the professor always carried with him. Alice reached in, took it and turned it over in her hands.

"It's not a book at all," said Alice. "It's a box." She pointed to a small hole hidden in the side of the box between the flaps of the page edges. "A keyhole. The pages are just fake."

"Can you pick that too?" Penelope asked.

Alice peered at the keyhole. It was smaller than she would have liked. Smaller locks could be tricky.

"How long have we been?" she asked.

"Four minutes?" said Penelope. "Maybe five? I'll go and keep watch. If the professor comes back towards the door I can stall him and warn you he's on the way. Lock the door behind me."

Alice smiled at her. Penelope was remarkably willing to throw herself into things. Alice watched her leave, locked the door and turned her attention to the box. She would have to listen to the delicate clicks of the lock's workings as well as keep one ear listening for Penelope's warning. She got to work quickly, but there was something different about this lock. It was so quiet and the mechanism so gentle that before long she found that she had tuned out the sounds around her, the rhythmic beat of the carriage wheels rattling against the rails, the gentle whooshing of the wind through the gap in the window and rain pattering against the glass. Alice pushed it all to the back of her mind and concentrated only on the tiny pins inside the lock.

After a few minutes, she felt the world rushing back in on her. Nothing was working.

"It won't move," she moaned, aware that her hands were beginning to shake from the tension. A memory pricked at the back of her head, of trying to add those stars to the spun sugar on her Eiffel Tower cake. The steady hand she had needed, the calm breaths, and the willingness to loosen her grip so that her hands did not stiffen and tremble. She closed her eyes, drew in deep breaths and felt herself relax. The first bar of the lock clicked.

After four clicks she was sure that she was close to opening the box, when the sound of Penelope's voice dragged her attention back to the compartment. She heard footsteps in the corridor outside, the sound of the professor's voice above Penelope's. Alice made one final turn with her pin and, with a click, the lid of the box popped open.

Penelope's voice, slightly raised, came through the door. "Oh, good evening, Professor, I was just coming to the bar. Do you think you could help me find something?" Hoping that Penelope could delay him, Alice snapped open the box.

On top of a coil of pearls and diamonds sat a platinum brooch with the biggest emerald Alice had ever seen, shaped like an egg and surrounded with yellow stones that might be yellow sapphires or, more probably, diamonds. A pair of ruby hairclips, slightly bent through being crammed next to an emerald-encrusted ring, peeked out from the pile in the corner of the box. Penelope had been right. The ruby hairclips, the brooch with an emerald as big as an egg – this was the jewel haul from the hotel at Le Touquet. Jake and Irving had nothing to do with it, but Penelope had been right that the thief was on the train – it was the professor.

Alice heard the professor's voice from the corridor.

"I'm sorry, young lady, but I'm very tired. I'm sure the staff will help you find it in the morning." She heard Penelope begin to object and then the door of the carriage rattled. The professor's key was in the lock.

Alice glanced round. Under the soft padding of its deep pillows, the banquette was solid lacquered wood to the floor and the luggage rack offered no hiding place. She looked at the open window with dismay and realised there was only one way out.

CHAPTER
FOURTEEN

For the second time in less than a week, Alice found herself clinging on to a windowsill by the tips of her fingers, but this time her feet balanced only on the narrow bar that ran the length of the train. She dug in tight with her fingers and tried not to panic as the train swung from side to side like a wild beast trying to tip her off.

She tried to think what Uncle Robert would advise, but instead it was her mother's voice that came to her. "*Stay calm,*" said Madame Éclair in that firm but soft voice she used when the pâtisserie was a whirl of activity and Alice was a frazzled mess trying to juggle too many jobs at once.

"*Stay calm,*" she repeated. The wind whipped past, stinging her eyes with raindrops and smuts from the engine. Alice buried her face in the side of the train carriage and blinked the pain away. The train was moving through the outskirts of a small town. Soon it would be back out in the countryside and running full pelt, and Alice would have no chance of holding on. She had to get back to Penelope's compartment as quickly as she could!

Steeling herself, Alice turned to look down the train. The wind slapped her face and whipped her fringe across her eyes, the rain plastering it to her forehead. She shook her head and, taking a deep breath, began to edge her way down the carriage, feeling for the narrow strip of wood that she was balanced on, her shoes slipping against the rain-soaked lacquer every time she moved. She could feel her heart beating fiercely in her chest and willed her hands to stop shaking as she gripped the edge of the windowsills. But with every step, the train was travelling further and further towards the edge of the town and her time was running out. Alice was halfway down the carriage when she saw a black void opening up before her, swallowing the front of the train, then the first carriage, then the second…

She cried out and crushed herself against the side of the train as it swept into the tunnel and she was covered in darkness and noise. As the sound of the engine roared and echoed off the walls, Alice had to fight a sudden impulse to cover her ears to protect them from the shrill scream of the train's whistle. She screwed her eyes shut against the hot choking smoke and held her breath till she felt the cold rush of air as they cleared the tunnel.

They were out in the country now, the train picking up speed. Alice willed herself to move more quickly, clawing her way along the carriage. The countryside whirled past her as, step by step, she covered the distance to Penelope's window. She pressed her face against the glass and peered through the sliver of a gap between the drawn curtains. She could see Penelope walking backwards and forwards inside the compartment, biting her fingernails, but Penelope did not see the face staring through the window. Tentatively, Alice peeled her fingers off the edge of the sill, but as the train lurched from one side to another, she changed her mind and clasped at the wood ever tighter. There was only one thing for it, and, wincing at how much this would hurt, Alice drew back her head and butted at the window.

It took several thuds before the curtains were drawn fully back and Penelope's shocked face stared back at her. Penelope sprang at the leather strap holding the window in place, let the glass fall and leaned out to grab hold of Alice. It was only as Penelope was hauling her through the window that Alice realised how much every sinew in her arms was screaming at her. She felt her shins scrape against the wood of the windowsill and then she was through and collapsing in a heap on the floor.

"What on earth did you think you were doing?" cried Penelope, leaning over and helping her on to the padded bench. She hurried to her luggage and brought back a soft tartan blanket, which she wrapped round Alice's knees, and then fetched a towel for her dripping-wet hair. As Penelope fastened the window shut, Alice found that her teeth were chattering.

"It was the only way out of the professor's compartment," she said. "You were right. There *is* a thief on board and the professor *is* up to something. *He's* the thief and I have proof."

Penelope's eyes widened, but as Alice reached inside the pocket of her uniform and drew out a single ruby hairclip, her look of excitement changed to one of disappointment. "Oh, is that all?" Penelope said.

Alice fought back a shiver of cold. "Well, of course not. There are piles of jewels in that box of his, all the ones you told me had gone missing at Le Touquet, but if I took it all then he would know that someone had been in his room. But this should be enough to get one of the stewards to listen to you. Its pair is in the box in his room. You recognise it, don't you? A ruby hairclip – the one that was stolen from that woman at the hotel. Tomorrow, present this to your father. Tell him that you recognise it from the haul taken in Le Touquet and that all the passengers must be searched."

Penelope bit her lip. "They wouldn't believe that," she said. "They'll suspect the staff. We're First Class, you see. They *always* believe us. It's not fair, but it's true. Pip Montague was travelling in the Alps and the police were told that someone on board had stolen some money and they hardly even *looked* in the First Class carriages, even though the woman sitting opposite her was *very* shifty, according to Pip."

Alice frowned. "Well then, you are going to have to lie," she said. "Tell them you found it peeking under the door of the professor's cabin."

"I would much rather you did it," said Penelope. "I'm no good at that sort of thing."

"Nonsense," declared Alice. "You've been brilliant! You sneaked past the stewards this afternoon, and you got the professor out of the way so I could search. And, like you said, you are an elegant young lady. I'm just staff. Besides, it was you who first spotted that the jewels might be on the train."

"Yes, but *I* thought it was Jake and Irving," said Penelope. "I wasn't much use really."

Alice leaned forwards. "We would never even have suspected there was a thief on board without you. You've got instinct, Penelope Fulmington, and so few people have that." She pressed the sparkling hairclip into Penelope's palm and leaned back on the comfortable banquette.

"You look totally done in," said Penelope. "Does your head hurt? You're not going anywhere till you feel strong again. Do you want me to fetch one of the stewards with some tea?"

Alice shook her head. There would be some very awkward questions asked if she was caught sitting dripping wet in one of the guest compartments. Far better just to sit quietly till she felt less like the room was swimming around her and she could trust her legs not to turn to jelly. Instead, she sat and thought about the papers tucked inside her uniform while Penelope bustled around the compartment, shaking out a pair of pyjamas and draping them over the small chair by the nightstand. Penelope crouched down and opened the vanity case that sat on the floor, took out a bundle of long cloths and hung them on the towel hook before running some water into the sink.

"What are you doing?" Alice asked, staring at her.

Penelope laughed. "Have you never seen someone roll their hair before? Pip Montague says it's out of fashion now and everyone who's anyone has a simple straight bob, but I like my hair like this." She cupped her hand to the delicate wave of hair that framed her face. Alice's own hair was resolutely straight in spite of her mother's attempts with the curling iron. Once Alice had reached ten, Madame Éclair had declared that a simple chin-length bob was the only answer to a thick mop of hair, and Alice had been despatched to the hairdresser to have her tresses chopped off.

"You're lucky to have such lovely hair," she said admiringly. Penelope beamed at her.

"I take good care of it. I like to try all the new products if I can. Last term, Pip read something in a fashion magazine that said egg was good for your hair, so she cracked a whole fresh egg over hers! But when she tried to wash it out, it scrambled and stuck to her like glue. It took *hours* to comb out."

Alice laughed. "*Maman* lets me wash mine in violet water sometimes," she said.

"Well, I like mine to curl, but Papa doesn't trust me with a curling iron," huffed Penelope, "so this is the next best thing – the old-fashioned way."

She smoothed her hair down so that it lay flat against her head. Then she dipped her fingers into the water and smoothed them down her hair.

"You take a fingerful of hair," she said, talking to Alice but looking at her reflection in the mirror, "and twist it into a coil, like so, then you wrap it in cotton and tie it good and tight till morning."

Penelope started to work her way round her head. Alice stared at her. Round and round each coil of hair went the fabric strips, like the dressings on a mummy, or the bandage that Alice's mother had put on her arm the first time she had used the great oven at *Vive Comme L'Éclair* on her own and had burned herself taking out a tray of shortbread, or... Alice felt a jolt of recognition.

I know what the hairpin is! she thought, clamping her hand over her mouth, so sure was she that she must have cried it out loud.

"Are you OK?" asked Penelope, pausing mid-coil. "You've gone awfully pale. Are you sure you haven't caught a chill or something?"

Alice nodded. She felt in her pocket for the hairpin. She could not wait to put her theory to the test.

A little over an hour later, Alice was sat at one of the tables in the dining carriage, fighting the tiredness that was settling in as the train rocked from side to side, speeding through the night. Outside, moonlight picked out the rolling hills and played over a stream that wound its way alongside the track. Alice had finally escaped from Penelope's worried care after assuring her that she felt well enough and must get some sleep, and Penelope's yawns had convinced her that her new friend would soon be fast asleep herself. Even then, Alice had not been able to escape until she promised to write to Penelope all about life in Paris and had been given Penelope's home address, and her school address, and the addresses of her parents' ski lodge and that of her aunt who lived somewhere called Hertfordshire, where Penelope said she was forced to spend "deathly dull Christmases".

Alice had chosen a table in the middle of the carriage where she could easily see the doors at either end in case anyone walked through. The room was thick with a sickly mix of perfume and cigars, so Alice had opened one of the windows to breathe in the fresh night air.

Alice took Stella's hairpin from her pocket. *A scytale.* Why hadn't she thought of it before? The answer to that was obvious. It was a cipher that Uncle Robert, in his notes, had warned her never to use for anything important. "Far too easy to decode," he had written. "Once you guess the diameter of the instrument, you have the key." Still, there was an elegance to a scytale, and it was one of the world's oldest ciphers so Alice was fond of it. She turned the hairpin over in her hand. Though at first sight it had looked perfectly smooth, Alice now noticed a break in the wood at one end, a narrow groove of about half a centimetre. *Just deep enough*, thought Alice, *to secure a slip of paper...*

So you are a spy after all, she thought. Only a spy would carry such an instrument. She glanced at the identity papers on the table next to her. Might this note give her a clue as to who these people really were?

Alice studied the pin carefully. She took her ever-present notebook from her pocket and scored a line down the edge of the paper, tore it away in a thin strip and began to transcribe the letters that she remembered from Stella's notebook.

E.F.N.I.I.U.D.E.G.G.F.S.H.E.A.S.T.E.M.A.R.S.I.F.E.
A.L.E

Alice scribed the message out on to the strip and then picked up the hairpin. She folded the end of the paper over and slotted it into the groove at the end of the pin.

"Please let this work," she whispered to herself. Then, just like Penelope had wrapped the cotton rag around her hair, Alice began to wrap the strip of paper around the pin, scanning the letters as they fell into place, searching for any emerging patterns.

It was as the paper was folding round the edge of

the pin for the third time that Alice spotted "EIG" forming along one side. The letters were slanted, but that could be due to her writing being a little too large. She wrapped the paper round twice more and "EIGHT" appeared. Alice gasped. Taking care to pull the paper as tightly as she could, she continued winding. A few minutes later she had the complete message:

"*Eight refugees and families safe.*"

Alice shook her head. Refugees? What did it mean? She glanced through the identity papers again, reading the professions of those listed. "A lie is dependent upon a core of truth," she heard Uncle Robert say. The names on the papers may be fake, but there would be details that were true. Mrs Johnson with her three children was a doctor. The elderly Professor Smith was a specialist in the law. There were three writers and a journalist, a schoolteacher and a nurse. They were professional people, just the sort who could be useful as spies, so why did Alice have the feeling that Stella's note was telling the truth?

Lawyers, writers, journalists. These were people who could make themselves very unpopular, and

Alice had heard the stories that were coming out of Germany. Stories about how the new people in power were treating anyone who disagreed with them. Stories about the dangers facing good German people who tried to stand up for those in trouble.

And here she was, jeopardising that.

Alice felt her stomach turn to ice. What would happen if these people were refused entry to safety because of her? She must get the papers back to Stella. She snatched up the scytale and began to unravel the paper from it. Her mind was whirling. How could Uncle Robert have got it so terribly wrong? How glad he would be that his Little Phantom had found out the truth while she could still put things right.

As Alice was gathering the papers together, the train began to slow and rock more noticeably as it approached a town, and Alice became aware of a shadow behind her, a breath on the back of her neck and the click of a gun.

She froze.

"Put the papers down," whispered a voice. There was something about it that was familiar, but Alice could not place it. She gave a short nod of her head and lowered the papers gently to the table.

"Good girl," continued the voice. "Now I am going to blindfold you and leave the carriage. If you move before I leave the train, I shoot. Do you understand?"

Alice nodded again. She winced as the figure leaned past her ear with a gloved hand to pick up one of the train's napkins, pulled it across her face and roughly tied it behind her head. Alice felt tears prick her eyes as the knot caught at her hair. She held her breath as the stranger picked up the papers, and she felt their arm brush against her chin. Then the fear in her solidified into rage and she leaned forwards and bit down hard on the hand that lay near her throat.

She heard the figure cry out. Her head was pulled to one side as her attacker wrenched their hand out of the glove, and then they stumbled past her and headed towards the door. Alice whipped the glove from her mouth and threw it to the table. She tugged at the blindfold but it was so tight around her head that she could not force it off.

As she grappled with the fabric, Alice became

aware of voices, low and urgent, arguing at the end of the carriage. There was the sound of scuffling and then a loud knock and more arguing. Alice gave one last try to tear the blindfold away and winced as it ripped out several hairs from the back of her head.

Alice saw Stella at the end of the carriage, dressed in her pyjamas and an outdoor coat, locked in a struggle with someone who had his back to her. All Alice could see were the dark curls of his hair above a high collar. Alice sprang from her seat and set off down the carriage.

By the time she reached them, the man had pushed Stella out into the corridor. Alice hurled herself at him and grabbed at the papers in his hand. The man lost his footing for a moment. His head whipped round and Alice cried out in shock as he faced her.

"Uncle Robert!"

Alice staggered back against the wall in shock, her head whirling. What was Uncle Robert doing on the train? Had he come to help her? Of course, he thought that the papers Stella had were helping the enemy, not France.

"Uncle Robert," she cried out. "She's not what

you thought..."

Her uncle ignored her. Free from his grasp at last, Stella reached a hand into her pocket, but Uncle Robert was too quick. His arm flew out and he dragged Alice to him.

"Don't do anything foolish," he said. Alice was about to say that she didn't understand, when she realised he was talking to Stella. Stella withdrew her hand from her pocket and held it aloft, the fingers spread wide to show that it was empty.

"Good girl," Robert Éclair muttered. "Now, you are going to get off the train. Do I make myself clear?" He motioned towards the door. Stella's eyes widened.

"You see, Alice," he murmured in Alice's ear. "I knew that you would be in danger. I boarded at Paris Lyon. The minute I finished talking with you on the phone I got in the car, motored across the city and took a seat in the Third Class compartment, just in case you needed me. I knew it was a mistake to mention this train to you. Of course, my Little Phantom would not resist being on board, but these are dangerous times, Alice. I realised I could not let you make such a treacherous journey alone and I was right. The minute I saw this woman threatening you, I knew I had to act."

"What do you mean, threatening her? It was you. I saw you!" Stella cried.

"My own niece?" Robert Éclair scoffed. "Rubbish!" Alice felt his grip on her arm tighten and he leaned closer to her ear. "Alice, you know that it wasn't me. It was her. Look, the gun is in her pocket. She was about to draw it again."

Alice turned her face so she could look him in the eye. Uncle Robert had been so dear to her when she was little. Though she knew he was capable of lying. His pretend death was proof of that. But she did not think that he would ever lie to *her*, and certainly he would not try to hurt her. Surely he must be telling the truth.

Uncle Robert moved to the train door and reached for the handle. "The train will slow as it pulls through Avignon," he said. "I'm not a complete monster. If you want to survive the fall, you should go now before it clears the station."

Alice gasped. Surely her uncle did not seriously expect Stella to jump from a moving train. She was about to object, when she noticed his hand on the door. It was gloved. The one around her waist was not. And Stella was not wearing gloves at all.

She saw her uncle follow her glance.

"Alice…"

"It *was* you," she gasped.

Alice was not sure who moved first. She was aware of her uncle's face hardening as he stared at her, of the sensation of being pulled towards the open door, the lights of the station as the train pulled alongside the platform, and of Stella's voice screaming at him to stop. And then she was falling, the night air rushing into her ears and the whistle of the train covering her screams.

CHAPTER
FIFTEEN

Alice hit the platform with a force that knocked the air out of her lungs, leaving her gasping for breath. She tried to sit up and winced as every bone in her body cried out in complaint, then laid back down on the ground, feeling hot tears spill down her cheeks. She had failed. Above her, the last blinking lights of the train disappeared round the curve of the line and the rattle of the carriages echoed into the silent night.

"I should have realised from your name," said a voice beside her in the dark. "Éclair. I thought it must be a coincidence."

Alice turned her head. A few metres away from her, Stella lay panting on the ground and clutching her ankle.

"You jumped," Alice said

"Don't be silly, you little fool. Your precious uncle caught me off guard and threw me out after you. Seeing him push you was a surprise, but then, after you betray your country, I suppose betraying family isn't too great a leap."

Alice winced. "He didn't betray his country. He was a hero."

"Oh yes, the great Robert Éclair," Stella scoffed.

"He's the biggest double agent France has ever had. For years he stole France's secrets and betrayed her agents. The man is responsible for goodness knows how many people being in prison or worse. And the minute he was discovered for the traitor he really was, he conveniently drowned in the Seine. I always suspected he was still alive, and now I have proof. And it looks like he also has a nasty little apprentice too. Or had, at any rate. Still, you'll be very useful to the authorities."

Alice saw Stella's hand go to her pocket and she froze as she heard the click of a gun.

"Nice of him to let me keep this," said Stella. "Perhaps he just wasn't bothered enough about you to care. Anyway, you're coming with me. And I *will* use this if I need to."

Alice stared at the gun. "I… I was trying to help France."

"Help France? Don't be ridiculous. You stole the papers. Those papers… They..." Stella reached out and gripped Alice's jacket. "Have you any idea what you have *done*!" The gun trembled in Stella's hand and Alice saw not just anger but fear in the woman's eyes.

"The people in the papers you stole are good people, fighting against ideas that could tear Europe apart. Albert published a volume of poems about freedom that angered his government. We told him we could get him and his little girl, Lise, to a safe place. Denise wrote an article in a paper that questioned whether the authorities were telling the truth. Hans, Elise, Adel: all of them hoping for new lives because where they live is not safe for them any more. Their children will be in danger. Their parents. You have betrayed all of them. You're a filthy little traitor and I should shoot you right here."

Before she could stop herself, Alice burst into tears. She had been so foolish. *Oh, clever, clever Alice Éclair, swanning around pretending to be a spy. You know NOTHING*, a voice in her head shrieked. She felt her chest tighten, and the night and the cold seemed to close in on her, suffocating her as she gasped for breath. With a howl, Alice let the hot tears spill down her cheeks.

"I – I didn't know," she wailed. "I thought they were spies – my uncle told me they were papers to help spies get into France, not people trying to escape danger... I didn't realise till I opened the packet and – and saw their faces."

Alice covered her face completely with her hands. She had never felt so ashamed, so worthless. She had thought she was some great saviour of France, but all along she had played into the hands of a man who was working for the enemy and endangering innocent lives. The faces of the little girls in the papers swam in front of her eyes. The kindly-looking man with the monocle stared at her, his face full of sadness. How could she ever make up for this?

She heard the gun click again and thought she was going to vomit with fear, but there was no explosion in the cold night and Alice realised that Stella had replaced the safety catch. She lowered her hands and met the woman's eye. Stella was glaring at her, but the gun had gone back into her pocket. "Get off the ground and tell me everything he told you," she said.

Alice clambered slowly to her feet, feeling her whole body shaking and not quite trusting her legs to hold her.

"He said I had to work out who the spy was and then take the papers and hold on to them till I got back to Paris. Then I was to take them straight to him. And I had to have them by the time the train reached Marseilles because that was where the spy was getting off."

"Well, that's not right," said Stella. "My contact is at Nice. He must have made a mistake."

"Why did he get on the train? Why take the papers from me at all? I would have given them to him in two days' time anyway. He didn't need to do any of this."

Stella sighed. "Robert Éclair always was a controller. There is no way he would have let you carry out this mission alone. Of course he was going to watch you."

Alice thought back to all the times that she'd thought she could hear her uncle's voice in her head, or feel that he was guiding her. It had felt like he was near, like she had never lost him. A chill ran through her. Was it actually because he'd been watching her all along, controlling her as if she was a marionette?

"And he's a coward," Stella continued. "He left you to do the really dangerous work so that he could just step in when it was safe and take the papers from you."

"But why?" asked Alice. "Why not just wait till I

got back?"

"Because you read them," said Stella. "He knows you're smart enough to have worked out that something didn't add up. And I'm betting he knew that once you realised what was really going on, you would want no part of it."

Alice felt the breath catch in her chest. "So, you believe me, then?"

"Yes," nodded Stella. "He had you stitched up. I'm sorry. You're a smart girl. You deserve better."

Alice shook her head violently. "I don't deserve anything," she muttered. "I've ruined everything."

"Yes, you have," Stella said. "But what you haven't yet learned, Mam'selle Éclair, is that in espionage, what is ruined can often be fixed if you have the right plan. We just need to come up with one."

Alice thought for a moment.

"Uncle Robert doesn't make mistakes," she said slowly.

"What?"

"You said he made a mistake, when he said he needed me to have that parcel by the time we reached Marseilles. But he's too clever for that. He had this all so well planned. If he wanted the papers to be with me by the time we reached Marseilles, then there must be a reason for that. I don't think he took the papers *just* because I read them. It might have meant he had to swipe them off me instead of getting them some other way, but he *always* intended to get the papers off me somehow, and before we reached Marseilles."

"So he would have them ..." said Stella.

"... to give to a contact," finished Alice. "*He* is heading for Marseilles."

"Mam'selle Éclair, I think you are right." Stella peered at her wristwatch in the moonlight. "Marseilles is over an hour away," she said. "And we have no transport."

Alice groaned. It was hopeless.

What was it that Stella had just said? *In espionage what is ruined can often be fixed if you have the right plan.* It was an echo of what her mother loved to say while trimming the edges off burned biscuits and crumbling the good part into cream for a dessert. *Nothing is ever wasted and nothing cannot be saved.* It was *Maman*'s motto, always useful when the milk soured and had to be used for scones, or when eggs curdled and had to be coaxed back into shape with a little extra flour, or…

Eggs!

"What time is it?" asked Alice.

"Time?" said Stella. "It's just after midnight."

"And we are just outside Avignon," murmured Alice. She scrambled to her feet.

"Yes, but—"

"The egg pallets on the train," said Alice. "They were from the same farm that supplies Minou's, the place we get ours from in Paris. It's the best place in the city. They get things from farms all over France – small farms, making the very finest ingredients. The same places that a train like the Sapphire Express would use."

"This is a charming insight into your work, Mam'selle Éclair," said Stella, "but I'm not sure—"

"The farm that supplies Minou's is somewhere just outside Avignon!" cried Alice. "I saw it on the egg pallet. And if they supply Paris, then there's a chance they supply Marseilles too and they will be heading to the city before daybreak."

"A slim chance," said Stella. "And how would we even find them?"

Alice cast her mind back to the pallet of eggs

in the kitchen of the Sapphire Express. She could still see that sketch of the outskirts of Avignon. She squeezed her eyes shut and studied it as if it was a map in front of her, following the road out of town, turning right at the mark of a cross...

She snapped her eyes open and smiled at Stella.

"I think I know where to go," she said.

Half an hour later, they were on the edge of a small farmyard. Alice peered at the house, looking for signs of life, and sighed with relief when she saw a flash of light behind one of the drawn curtains. The farmer was rising. Alice leaned over the gate. Her hand hovered above the latch.

"What are you waiting for?" asked Stella. "We've come this far already."

Alice took a breath. "What if I'm wrong?" she asked in a small voice.

"I'm afraid that being wrong is not an option, Alice," said Stella, and Alice sensed that she was keeping her voice as soft as possible. "It's not just that those papers were a route out of danger for those families. If they fall into the wrong hands, then it will be easy for the enemy to track down our forger. If they uncover our network, then a lot of people helping and hiding refugees could be in grave danger."

Alice bit her lip. Stella leaned over and placed a hand on hers.

"So we get them back, Alice Éclair. And if you think that the key to getting them back lies in a muddy farmyard, well, I'm prepared to trust you. The girl who can decipher my codes deserves nothing less. Which reminds me..."

She removed her hand and turned it so that it was palm up.

Alice looked at her in puzzlement and then it dawned on her what Stella was asking for.

She reached into her pocket and dropped the hairpin into Stella's waiting hand. Then she unlatched the gate and stepped into the farmyard.

CHAPTER
SIXTEEN

"I think you're going to have to rap louder than that, Alice," murmured Stella after Alice had tapped twice on the farmhouse door.

Alice knocked again, more firmly this time, wincing as the sound echoed in the quiet night. She shuffled from side to side, stamping her feet and wishing that she was wearing something other than her uniform. Now that they had stopped walking, she was beginning to notice how cold the night air was.

She glanced at Stella in her pyjamas and slippers. Stella was at least wearing her warm overcoat, but her dainty pumps were now caked in mud, which was soaking into the bottom of her silk pyjamas.

Alice was about to knock once more when she heard noises on the other side of the door and a latch being pulled back. The door swung open and a bleary-eyed man peered at them from a warm parlour. Alice looked longingly at the fire over his shoulder and, as the smell of freshly cooked crêpes hit her nose, she felt her stomach groan. Stella nudged her sharply in the small of the back.

"I... That is, we ... work for the Sapphire Express," started Alice. "I believe you supply them with provisions for the kitchen?"

The man eyed her curiously. Alice supposed that she must look quite strange, standing on his doorstep in the middle of the night quizzing him about his food sales.

"Your eggs, for example?" prompted Alice. The man's face cleared a little and he nodded.

"Ah, yes," he said, opening the door a little wider. "We provide eggs to all the finest restaurants in France. We keep Faverolles here, you see, Mam'selle, the finest chickens in the region."

Alice caught sight of Stella's face and coughed to prevent herself from smiling.

"We find ourselves accidentally separated from our train," Alice explained, reminding herself that the easiest lies to tell were the ones that were closest to the truth. We thought that maybe we could rejoin at Marseilles, if anyone was going in that direction and could offer us a lift?"

The man looked back at the mantlepiece in his parlour where a clock stood, and he frowned. "Well, I don't know, Mam'selle. I doubt you would get to Marseilles for the early train. I think your best bet is to wait till it comes back through Avignon and catch it then."

Alice shook her head. "No use, I'm afraid." She stopped. *Why* was it no use? Think. What would Uncle Robert advise? No. He was no longer allowed to talk to her. She half turned to look at Stella, but that would not do either. *You can't rely on other people all your life*, she told herself. From now on, she would learn from herself. She had, after all, managed to get on to the Sapphire Express without anyone else's help once already. Of course, then she had used the cake she baked to get their attention... That was it!

"Monsieur, I'm sorry, but I need to be on that train," said Alice. "I will be baking a cake for the birthday of a Vicomte from Monaco. You see, I work at *Vive Comme L'Éclair,* the finest pâtisserie in Paris. Perhaps you have heard of us? We won the Blue Riband at the *Pâtisserie Spectaculaire* four years running."

The farmer's eyes widened at this and he swung the door open wide enough to usher Alice and Stella in to the kitchen.

"Well," he said, "we're meant to be heading that way anyway. I suppose Gabriel might be able to push the car to its limits to get you down there. A Vicomte, you say? Take a seat by the fire and I'll tell that boy to hurry himself up."

As the man hurried off up the narrow stairs of the farmhouse, Stella and Alice collapsed into two very comfortable armchairs by the crackling fire. Stella raised an eyebrow at Alice. "A Vicomte?"

"Shush," said Alice. "I made him up. People always react to a title, have you noticed?"

"Have I *not*!" retorted Stella. "I myself have been a countess, a baroness and a minor duchess more times than I can count. I was meant to be playing the part of an English lady only this week, but plans changed and I had to go to a house party as plain old Gina."

Alice started. She remembered the mess of the room at the mansion in Paris, the scarves looped round the furniture handles. She knew now what Stella's compartment on the train had reminded her of.

"You're Gina Mannitoc!" she cried. "*La Renarde*!"

Stella sat up straight in her chair and shushed her.

"You!" she hissed. "It was you who took my microfilm!"

"And I gave it to Uncle Robert! That was how he knew that someone would be on the train with the papers. Oh, Stella, this really is all my fault."

Stella leaned over and took Alice's hand. "No," she said firmly. "The only fault and blame here lies with your uncle and those he is in league with. You have acted as honourably as you could. You were lied to, that's all. You didn't know."

Alice opened her mouth to answer, but before she could, a boy of about eighteen came stumbling down the stairs, pulling a jacket on and complaining about being dragged out of bed too early. The farmer followed close behind.

"Stop your whining, boy. You can have breakfast when you get to Marseilles. These ladies have an important mission for you. And we never let down a lady, do we?"

The boy locked eyes with Stella who, even after trudging through the countryside covered in mud, still looked more glamorous than most women Alice had ever met. He blushed a deep red and muttered something about how it would be a pleasure.

Five minutes later, Stella, Alice and the boy called Gabriel were crammed together on the long front seat of a small green van, rattling through the gates of the farmyard.

"If we get there by five," Alice calculated, "we can be on the platform for when the train pulls in."

"It'll be pushing it," said Gabriel, swinging the van on to a track off the side of the road. "But I know a few short cuts."

They bounced down the track with Gabriel expertly spinning the wheel to take the corners without slowing down. Alice glanced out of the window at the hedgerows flashing by. The sky was an inky blue peppered with stars, and the moon bathed everything in soft, shimmering light. Alice was vaguely aware of Stella striking up a conversation with Gabriel, talking ten to the dozen to cover the boy's evident shyness. She rested her head against the door of the van and closed her eyes for just a second, lulled by the rocking sensation and the exhaustion of the night.

CHAPTER
SEVENTEEN

Alice woke to the acrid smell of burning prickling in her nose and the snap of cold morning air biting her face. She blinked as her eyes squinted into the rising sun, shining through the van's windscreen. They had stopped moving.

"Where are we?" she asked, turning to Stella, but the seat beside her was empty, the driver's door left ajar. She leaned forwards, shielding her eyes against the sun, and saw Stella and Gabriel outside. The engine's cover was folded back over the front of the van and they were both staring into it. Smoke billowed out into Gabriel's grease-stained face.

Alice opened her door and jumped down to the ground, wincing slightly. Clearly her arms remembered that she had hung off the side of a train the night before. Every muscle in them was taut and painful. Alice rolled her shoulders to try to crack some life back into them as she rounded the front of the van and joined Stella.

"The radiator's cracked," Stella said, waving at the engine with one hand while the other covered her nose. "Gabriel has more water, but it will just steam straight out of it."

Alice stared at the engine. Gabriel had wrapped a

cloth around his hand and was dabbing at the source of the smoke. He shook his head and glanced at Stella.

"Really sorry, ladies, but it's done for. It won't run with a cracked radiator. And I'm not sure how we're going to get back home, let alone get on to Marseilles."

"Is there really nothing you can do?" Alice pleaded.

"It needs fixing with a good sealant and I don't carry that in the van," he said. He looked at Stella and then turned and gave the van's tyre a hefty kick.

"There must be something," Alice insisted. "We can't just give up." She looked desperately at Stella. This couldn't be it, could it? After everything they had been through, she refused to be defeated by a crack in a van engine. There was too much at stake!

"Alice, you did your best," Stella started, reaching out a hand for her shoulder, but Alice shook her off.

"We never give up," exclaimed Alice. "We put this right. You said that, remember? Well, we can't put it right if we're stuck out here in the countryside, can we?"

"We *will* right it," Stella said. "But not today.

Today we have to accept that we won't make that train on time. Like Gabriel said, he doesn't have what we need to fix this."

Alice opened her mouth to protest, but Stella was right. She turned away and bit her lip, hot tears pricking at the edge of her eyes. Uncle Robert had won. *Well, I hope you feel foolish, Alice Éclair,* she thought to herself. *All those grand ideas about being a master spy and you're stuck in a broken-down van with nothing but hundreds of eggs.*

Alice paused. An image had just flashed into her mind. Penelope telling her about a girl scraping egg off her hair. She thought about how quickly her mother had to work to stop the eggs in the bakery from sticking to the iron pans. "*A moment too long and they stick like glue,*" Madame Éclair would say.

"That's it!" Alice cried, turning to Stella. "I know how we can fix the radiator. Eggs!"

"Alice, please..." Stella began. "Not more eggs!"

"No, listen. If we break some over the engine, then the heat of the metal will cook them and they'll seal the break. Egg works just like glue if you heat it quickly enough."

Alice looked from Stella to Gabriel, who had lifted

his head and was looking at her thoughtfully.

"Well, it's worth a try," he said. "We've got nothing else."

Gabriel hurried to the back of the van and returned with a pallet of eggs.

"Here goes nothing," he said, picking up one of the glossy brown eggs and breaking it over the radiator. There was a hiss and a smell like breakfast. Gabriel worked quickly, adding more eggs till the steam rising from the engine started to die down. He twisted open a cap on one side and poured in water from a small tin bottle, then resealed it and stepped back. They watched as the egg bubbled and popped and finally congealed into a burned gluey mess on top of the metal. Gabriel closed the lid of the engine and nodded at them.

"Let's see if she holds," he said. "Hop back in."

Alice crossed her fingers so hard that they ached as she clambered back into the front of the van. Stella leaned over and gave her elbow a squeeze. Gabriel took a deep breath and held it as he turned the key in the ignition ... and the engine sprang into life.

"Please, please please..." muttered Alice as the

van trundled along the road. She was watching the engine like a hawk for signs of steam or smoke, but not a single puff escaped its metal casing. They reached a corner and swung on to a wide, straight road, and Gabriel gave a whoop of triumph.

Stella laughed. "I cannot believe that the day is about to be saved because you know more about the French egg trade than any other girl in France, Alice Éclair!" she said.

"Well," said Gabriel, "Papa always said that our eggs were the best in the business. Just wait till I tell him about *this*. He'll be selling them to every garage from Avignon to Monte Carlo!"

He threw them into third gear and they sped off towards Marseilles.

The station clock was chiming five by the time the van pulled up outside. Stella leaned across the seat and gave Gabriel a peck on the cheek, which stunned him into silence. Alice grinned her thanks and jumped down to the ground. They hurried through to the platform, Stella pulling her coat around her to hide the pyjamas underneath. Alice pulled off her white jacket, now covered in mud and grease, and hoped that the rest of her uniform underneath looked enough like a day dress.

The platform was quiet, as was to be expected, given the time. An elderly man was feeding the pigeons from a paper bag full of bread rolls, and an exhausted-looking woman with more children than she had hands was trying to keep order in a group clearly excited for their holidays. At the other end of the platform, a man in a guard's uniform was sweeping dust on to the tracks. A smartly dressed man reading a paper drew his feet away from the guard's broom and muttered something that made the guard glare at him and move away.

"Is the contact likely to be armed?" Alice asked.

Stella nodded. "Very probably," she said. "We will have to be careful."

"The train will be here soon," Alice said. "What do we do when the contact turns up? Wait for Uncle Robert to approach them?"

Stella pursed her lips. "What makes you think that they need to arrive?"

"What?"

"Look again, Alice."

Alice felt her heart give a sudden thump. The

agent was already here. They were out on the platform and Stella had spotted them.

She looked again at the people on the platform. What was she missing? She stared at the man with the paper bag, at the neat cut of his flannel suit and comfortable brown brogues. His hands were gnarled but gentle as he placed a morsel of bread down for a shy one-legged bird sheltering behind the bench leg.

She turned her attention to the young family nearby, but it seemed very unlikely that the woman busily organising her small troupe into an ordered line and doling out handkerchiefs and breakfast brioche would be awaiting a secret agent. Both she and the old man were, Alice thought, unlikely suspects.

My money's on the man with the paper, thought Alice. *The perfect disguise if one wants to sit quietly on a train station and wait for another agent to turn up.* She began to size up the man. He was wearing an expensive-looking well-cut suit, and the glint of light from below his cuffs suggested jewelled cufflinks. His hair was slicked back with rather too much brilliantine and his shoes were polished to perfection.

"His *shoes*!" she murmured.

Stella leaned forwards. "Yes. Whose shoes?"

Alice's head whipped round to the station guard, now emptying his dustpan into a bin at the end of the platform. He wore the drab black serge uniform of all the other guards, but while they had sensible, steel-toed boots on to protect their toes from runaway trolleys and falling luggage, he was wearing glossy black patent brogues with the most fashionable almond-shaped toes. Alice looked more closely at his face and noticed what she had missed before, the way his eyes darted around the platform, the tiny muscle in the side of his jaw that twitched with the tension of keeping up the facade.

In the distance, she heard a whistle sound and the huff of an engine. The rails by the platform edge began to sing. In a moment the Sapphire Express would pull in and her uncle would deliver the papers into this man's hands.

Alice glanced around.

"Alice, what are you looking for?" Stella's voice was low, but full of warning.

Alice ignored her. She had seen what she needed.

Someone had left a newspaper on a table outside the small café in the middle of the platform. She grabbed hold of it, and then rifled through the deep pocket of her uniform for the one notebook she had saved from the train.

"I've got an idea," she whispered, tearing a sheet of plain paper from her notebook. She folded the newspaper into a small bundle and wrapped it in the paper. Then she took the ribbon from her hair and tied it round the bundle.

Stella stared at the parcel.

"Alice, no. This won't be safe."

"None of this ever is, is it," said Alice and, ignoring Stella's protests, she set off across the platform.

The man dressed as a guard was looking out towards the incoming train. Alice, walked past the benches and piles of luggage, taking care not to draw attention to herself. The sound of the train grew louder and louder until, with a great roar and a screech of the protesting brakes, it was upon them, filling the platform with steam and heat. For a precious second Alice could not see the man. Which meant he could not see her.

Alice slipped quickly to one of the doors of the

train, opened it and then slammed it shut as though she had just got out, and walked quickly across the platform towards the man. She noticed him begin to slouch his shoulders a little more as she drew near and he affected a tuneless whistle. Alice hoped that she looked more collected than she felt. Her knees threatened to buckle with every step and she was sure that her heart was beating loud enough to echo off the station's roof. She drew in deep breaths.

Around her the passengers bustled to get on to the train. The woman with the children caught a passing steward for help with her luggage. The old man stood up from his bench and embraced a woman from Third Class who dashed across the platform to him. Alice tuned out the slamming of doors and the heat of the smoke and steam and focused on what she had to do.

You are Alice Éclair, she told herself. *You have come this far and you are going to see it through. You solved Stella's puzzles, you saved the day when we were stuck out in the countryside, and you can beat this man.*

"Can I help you, Mam'selle?"

With a start, Alice realised that she had almost

walked into the man. She jumped back and then, remembering herself, she drew her shoulders down and willed herself to stay calm. But her mind was racing. Were there code words to share? Was there a signal that she should know in order to convince him that she was on his side? Stella was right, this was going to be a disaster and Alice found that all of her words had deserted her. She was tempted to draw on Uncle Robert's wisdom. He was bound to have taught her something that could be of use right now, but she was determined not to. He was not allowed to speak to her any more.

The man stared at her and Alice felt her toes curl. *Think*, she told herself. *Say something. Anything.*

Anything was better than silence.

Or was it?

Alice thought about Stella. About that look that came over the woman's face when she was listening for information. It was a look that said, "I am in control and need not say anything. I will just let you talk." She thought about how keen Penelope was to share everything she knew; all Alice had had to do was listen. Sometimes, offering people a silence meant they would fill it. Silence had power.

Alice fixed the man with a steady gaze. She let her eyes flick to the parcel tucked under one arm, and then back to meet his eye. There was a pause and Alice held her breath, hoping that her nerve would not break.

The man took a step towards Alice. She felt him brush against her elbow and then he was walking quickly across the platform away from her, his brush discarded on the ground. Alice looked down at her elbow and saw that the parcel had gone. Her head swam a little. She heard the guard's whistle and, with another great blast of steam that flew to the glass roof of the station and then billowed down, blocking everything from view, the Sapphire Express began to pull out on its way to Nice.

Moments later, Stella was by Alice's side.

"Alice, I should scold you for taking such a risk, but you did it. He believed you. Now we just have to hope that he doesn't open that parcel, find yesterday's newspaper in it and come back here looking for us. I have to know, though. How did you convince him you were his contact?"

Alice smiled.

"I just let him assume."

Stella looked at her quizzically. Alice started to laugh, relief at having faced down the enemy contact catching up with her. But as she looked over Stella's shoulder, the laugh died on her lips.

"Hello, Alice," said Robert Éclair.

CHAPTER EIGHTEEN

Stella whipped round to face Robert, placing herself between him and Alice. Alice noticed her hand go to her pocket and remembered that Stella carried a gun.

"You're too late!" Alice spat at him. "Your contact has gone. And you're going to hand the papers over to us instead."

Uncle Robert laughed.

"And why would I do that, Alice? That was one contact, but there are others. You can't stop the inevitable. You would have learned that, had you kept up your training."

"Why would I want to train with you now?" she retorted. "Now I know what a liar you are. You were never on France's side."

"Don't speak too soon, Alice," he said calmly. "I'm sure we can come to an arrangement. I can offer you considerably better rewards than your current associate, for a start."

He drew the papers from one of the deep pockets of his greatcoat and waved them in the air. Alice caught a glimpse of the faces on them and winced.

"Do you know what is in these, Alice?" he asked.

Alice nodded. "Families. Families you are going to

hand over to people who will harm them. I thought you were on *our* side."

Her uncle paused, then he threw back his head and laughed.

"All this talk of *sides*. Oh, Alice, do you think the world is truly so simple? I'm not on any side. Well, perhaps the side with the most money. What's in these papers is money. There are people who will pay me very well for the information in here."

Alice saw her uncle's eyes gleam. There was something ugly and frightening in them. She had thought him the greatest spy in France. Had it really just been about who would pay most for whatever information he could get hold of?

He yawned and fixed Alice with a derisive smirk. "Well, we appear to be at a stalemate. I won't give you these papers and you, I suspect, won't leave without them, and we both have guns. What to do?"

Alice's mind raced. He was right. What could she possibly offer him? What was it that he wanted to protect more than anything? Tears pricked at the corners of her eyes as she realised that a few days ago she would have assumed that the answer to that question was "her". What a fool she had been.

And then it came to her.

Himself.

What Uncle Robert valued above everything else was staying dead.

"If you hand them over," said Alice, "I'll keep your secret."

She heard Stella gasp.

"You can stay dead," Alice continued. "Stay in hiding. I know the truth now. Everyone else truly thinks you are dead. Well, you're dead to me now too. Hand the papers over and I give you my word that I won't tell the authorities the truth."

"Alice, no!" hissed Stella. "This is our chance to put him away for good."

"And lose the chance to rescue those children," said Alice. The small faces in the identity papers sprang into her mind and she knew, in this moment, that she would do anything to protect them.

"You can't trust him, Alice," warned Stella. "He's as slippery as his old code name."

Alice glanced round at her for just a second. A freight train was pulling noisily through the station, its trucks packed with coal rattling against the rails. What did Stella mean by slippery? At once the truth dawned on her.

"The eel! *You* are *L'Anguille*! But you said *L'Anguille* was the spy I was chasing!"

Her uncle made a sardonic bow. "My little joke," he said. "You couldn't possibly understand how boring being dead is. And, after all, it really was me you were up against, not this woman. I can't say I'm not impressed by how much of it you worked out, though, Alice. You're a clever girl. So you won't be surprised if I do this." And with one swift movement he lifted his arm and flung the parcel on to the top of one of the passing trucks.

"NO!"

Alice bounded towards the train, but her uncle and Stella were there before her. Uncle Robert leapt on to the side and scrambled to the top, laughing. Stella caught at the truck behind, her shoe slipping against the wood. Alice leapt up behind her and deftly swung herself up, rolling on to the heap of coal. She leaned over, offered Stella her arm and dragged her to safety just as the truck rolled within centimetres of a wall.

Alice looked to the next truck. Her uncle was trying to steady himself on the rolling nuggets of coal, pitching forwards as they shifted beneath him. Alice crawled to the front of the truck and looked down. The rails flashed beneath the coupling between the trucks.

"Careful, Alice, this stuff is impossible to stand on," warned Stella.

Alice nodded. She felt the coal slipping beneath her and ground her hands and knees down into it to try to steady herself. She waited till there was a straight run of track where she would not risk being thrown around as the truck swung round bends. Holding her arms out for balance, she dug in her heels and rose to her feet. She saw her uncle pause. They stared at one another. Then Alice bent her knees, braced herself and leapt, landing in a heap on the truck, two metres from him.

Uncle Robert staggered back, but he kept his balance.

"I can't let you have them, Alice," he said. "I need the money. And I'm a marked man now. If the people I work for don't get these papers, I'll be a dead one. Besides, I can hardly go back home now you know the truth. Whatever you say, I can't risk it. *Trust no one, remember.* Not even family. If only you'd remembered. You can't say I didn't warn you, Alice. It's a new life for me somewhere. And new lives need funds."

Alice clambered to her feet. She took a step towards her uncle.

"You could join us," she said. "Come back home. We'll talk to the authorities."

Her uncle laughed bitterly. "Prison wouldn't suit me, Alice. You've no idea what I've done. What we've done."

A cold chill swept through Alice.

We.

All the spying, all the little jobs he had sent her on. She'd been helping France's enemies all along. The thought made her sick.

"What have you turned me into?" she said.

Uncle Robert smiled. "The best little spy France never had."

"NO!" Alice shouted.

Her uncle laughed. It was a cruel laugh that cut through Alice. All those years of playful crossword puzzles and the pride he had shown in her when she caught on to a cipher sooner than he expected. Had he been planning this even when she was little?

Using her to betray her own country? Well, she wouldn't let him this time!

Alice staggered forwards, but it was hopeless. The coal slipped beneath her feet, threatening to throw her over the side of the wagon. She heard her uncle laugh once more. Alice glanced at the narrow wooden planks that formed the sides of the truck. She threw her weight sideways and slid down the mound of coal towards the edge. Behind her, she heard a gasp and, looking back, saw Stella, her eyes wide with alarm.

Alice kicked off her shoes. This would be easier if she was on something solid. She placed a foot on the narrow strip of wood, curling her toes slightly for grip. Then, gritting her teeth and feeling for balance, she slid her other foot in front of her. She looked dead ahead, ignoring the ground rushing by beneath her, and stepped forwards.

The train was nearing a bend. She *must* get to Uncle Robert before that. She moved more quickly. She heard her uncle mutter something and the skittering of the coal as he stepped away from her and lost his balance. The engine at the front of the train pulled round the bend. Alice was a few steps from her uncle. As the truck reached the bend and swung into it, she leapt towards him. Uncle Robert swiped at her, but she was too quick for him, fuelled with anger and the hurt of betrayal. Alice side-stepped the blow and grabbed at the parcel of papers in her uncle's hand. He pulled back. Their eyes locked. The track evened into a long, curved sweep, the truck jolted to one side and Alice felt herself falling backwards on to the pile of coal with the parcel clasped in her hand. She heard a cry from Stella and, lifting her head, realised that Uncle Robert was no longer there.

"No, oh no!" she cried, scrambling to the side of the truck. She looked over the edge with dread, expecting to see his crushed body beneath the wheels of the train.

"Alice, over there!" shouted Stella, pointing to a bank by the side of the track. Uncle Robert lay on his back, moving, alive. Alice watched him grow smaller and smaller as the train sped away. Then she looked down at the parcel in her hands.

"I have the papers!" she shouted to Stella, hugging them to her chest. She felt tears pricking at her eyes. She never wanted to let this precious parcel out of her sight.

"Of course you do! You're quite a talented young lady, Alice." Stella cried. "With the right teacher… Well, perhaps next time we will get the papers *and* the spy."

Through her tears, Alice stared at her.

"Next time?"

Stella arched an eyebrow.

"I don't think we've seen the last of you, Mam'selle Éclair."

CHAPTER
NINETEEN

Alice stepped off the funicular carriage at the top of Montmartre and stared out across the city. It was late September and, though it sometimes felt like her adventure on the Sapphire Express had been months ago, it had only been six weeks. Instead of the tourists that filled the city in July and August, the funicular had been packed with art students, arms laden with portfolios, who were making a pilgrimage to the studios of Monet.

She tucked her sketchbook under her arm and headed for the café that Stella had mentioned in her last note. She was early, but before they met, Alice had plans to sketch Montmartre's basilica of Sacré-Coeur for a bride who had planned a winter wedding and wanted a cake based on the white-domed church that watched over the city.

Alice sat down at a table with a good view of the church and began to sketch. She had made a start on the detail of the roof when a newspaper dropped on to her open sketchbook.

"I thought you would like to read the story on page three," Stella said with a smile, dropping into the chair opposite and waving at one of the waiters.

Alice picked up the newspaper and turned to a

picture of a smiling girl shaking hands with a portly man in a well-cut suit and a large mayoral chain. The caption above read *British Schoolgirl Captures Jewel Thief Scourge of the Elite.*

"Oh, good on Penelope!" said Alice.

"Quite a remarkable young lady," said Stella. "Jake and Irving are in the paper too, if you want to know how they are doing. Page seven."

Alice found the article. A picture of Jake and Irving in top hat and tails filled half the page under a headline that said *Smash Hit of Hopper Brothers.* "Jake and Irving Hopper have made a splash in their return to Le Touquet, just six months after the brothers' first disastrous tour was cut short when, rumour has it, they fell out over *a certain young socialite* and refused to appear on stage with one another for their final night."

Alice smiled to herself. So *that* was why Jake and Irving didn't like to mention Le Touquet. They were just embarrassed, and maybe still a little cross with one another.

"What are you smiling about?" asked Stella.

Alice was about to tell her, but stopped herself. She would have to confess that Penelope's suspicions had first fallen on Jake and Irving, and that seemed mean.

"Nothing," she said, folding the paper up. "It's just nice to see them doing well."

"Well, look, I know we are here to talk about the next mission," said Stella. "But there is someone I want you to meet."

She nodded towards a man of about thirty who was walking down the cobbled street, pointing out the sights to a child beside him. Alice peered at them. They looked familiar, but Alice was sure she had not met them. Then the child spotted a squirrel dashing down the trunk of a tree and turned her face, full of glee, towards her father. Alice gasped.

"But that's..."

Stella nodded. "I thought you would like to meet them."

"They got out," Alice breathed. "You got them out."

"*We* got them out," Stella said. "Albert and Lise are safe now. He can write freely here, and they are thinking about going to London. They have family there."

Alice whisked away the tears that sprang to her

eyes. The man and his daughter were mounting the steps towards the café. Alice waved at the little girl and she waved back.

"You must stop all this endless blaming of yourself, Alice," Stella said firmly. "You trusted your uncle, and why shouldn't you have? He was family. But he was also a manipulative, bad man. And when you knew that truth – well, you put it right. Day by day, we are putting it right. And I promise you, Alice, we will track him down. He can't escape you for long, for all he underestimates his Little Phantom."

Alice shook her head. "The Little Phantom was his codename for me. I don't want it any more. I've chosen my own."

She slipped a hand into her pocket and drew out a small navy notebook. She let her finger trace the image she had asked the stationer to emboss into the front of it when she had decided who she was going to be from now on. A jagged flash of silver.

"A lightning bolt," said Stella.

Alice nodded. "I've always loved that my name means lightning. I don't want to be a phantom in the shadows. I want to be a flash of light, something powerful and full of life."

Stella nodded approvingly. "I can't think of any name that suits you better," she said.

Stella turned to greet Albert and Lise. Alice dropped the notebook back into her pocket. Tomorrow they could begin the work of tracking down Uncle Robert. Tomorrow she would make the first marks in that new notebook and become The Lightning Bolt. Tomorrow she would turn her mind to codes and ciphers and lies.

Today, she was Alice Éclair, the finest young pastry chef in all of Paris, and there was cake to be eaten.

Acknowledgements

Spies, codes and ciphers have always fascinated me. Disappearing inks, secret identities and messages hidden in codes all appeal to my love of puzzles and pretending. After taking a trip to the codebreaking centre at Bletchley Park in 2019, I decided I *had* to write a spy book and I wanted it to be full of ciphers that my readers could try to solve themselves.

As well as the amazing codebreakers of Bletchley, this book has been inspired by other real, brave people. Among them are the passport officers and diplomats across the world who saved refugees in danger in the 1930s by stamping passports and visas and helping them get forged passports that would see them to safety.

I'm so grateful for all the help I have had in writing this book. Thank you first of all to Joanna Moult, my amazing agent, who championed Alice from the start and who makes me believe in myself and my writing. Thank you to my wonderful editor, Fiona Scoble, without whom this book would be the poorer and the French would be much less accurate. I owe you both lots of cake. Thank you to everyone at Nosy Crow, especially Nic Theobald and Elisabetta Barbazza, whose cover designs are as gorgeous as Alice's cakes. And of course, huge thanks to Beatriz Castro, whose beautiful cover art brought Alice and her world to life perfectly.

Much love, too, to my gorgeous family and friends, to my Skylark Crew and Prime Writers for keeping spirits up and being the funniest and most supportive writing crews in the world, and to my workmates who I have missed so much these past two years. Thank you also to Richard Long, Richard Shipman and the lovely crew at Corris Railway, for answering many questions about steam trains.

As always, the biggest thanks to my tea maker, cheerleader, best friend and husband Neil. This book is dedicated to you. To solve the cipher, check inside your wedding ring. xxx